PRAISE FOR ALYSSA RICHARDS

THE HAUNTING OF ALCOTT MANOR is a fascinating tale of tragedy, ghosts, and soulmates. Mystery fans will enjoy this heroine's efforts to track down clues — both tangible and ghostly — while trying to find the truth about a woman's death. Romance fans will adore this match-up of a strong heroine and an enigmatic yet endearingly charming and earnest hero. I look forward to reading the next book in this tantalizing ALCOTT MANOR series." Fresh Fiction Review, THE HAUNTING OF ALCOTT MANOR

"Having read Alyssa Richards other books, I knew I was in for a treat, even though this was a slightly different genre. And gothic suspense being one of my absolute favorites, I was extremely psyched to read this book. Fortunately, everything that I anticipated about how good this book would be, and how much I would enjoy it, came true.

At first glance, this might appear to be your average haunted house story. But in the hands of this very capable, and highly readable author, it becomes so much more. The haunting was unique and the story revolving around the haunting was very intriguing. I totally did not anticipate the way the story was going or how it was going to end up. This was a great first entry in a new genre that I hope the author will continue. This book, as well as everything else this author has written, comes highly recommended." — DT

Chantel, book reviewer, THE HAUNTING OF ALCOTT MANOR

"Man oh man! Alyssa Richards has seriously outdone herself with this trilogy. It encompasses love, passion, deception, heartache, reality and alternate reality. Just stunning from start to finish. This trilogy is awesome. If you're looking for a paranormal romance that's focused around psychics and time travel, definitely grab this trilogy. It's simply amazing!" —*Nay's Pink Bookshelf, THE FINE ART OF DECEPTION SERIES*

5.0 out of 5 stars "Now this is what I'm talking about...absofreakingamazing!

"It's authors like Ms. Richards that really opened up the portals to my world, and instilled/nurtured within me a love for reading. Hook, line and sinker you are pulled fast and hard into her storylines and are wrecked when you've reached the end...you just don't want it to be over. The Haunting of Alcott Manor is no different and has a wonderful mix of gothic suspense/mystery with a titter of romance that will captivate you..and the end...omg I so didn't see that coming. What a stunning conclusion!"
—*Amazon Reviewer, THE HAUNTING OF ALCOTT MANOR*

5.0 out of 5 stars That ending...!? Are you kidding me?!
"Like others, I'm sure, I've read hundred(s) of these types of books. This was a great read, great twists and turns. ...and the end...? WOW! What's really getting me right now though? Henry and Gemma at still with me....days after I've finished the book! I cried with them, I loved with them, and they touched me deeply! Great job! (This is the first time I

have been inspired enough to write a review, too!)" *Amazon Book Reviewer, THE HAUNTING OF ALCOTT MANOR*

"A MURDER AT ALCOTT MANOR is very definitely a thrill-a-minute tale of evil trying to keep a stranglehold on the living. This is a perfect book for readers who enjoy non-stop action and suspense with a dash of sexy. ...This story will appeal to readers who love suspense, the paranormal, and everyday people who become unexpected heroes. Hope to read more gothic tales of love and paranormal peril by Alyssa Richards in the future." Fresh Fiction Review, A MURDER AT ALCOTT MANOR

Be the first to know about Alyssa Richards' next novel, sign up here: www.AlyssaRichards.com
and follow her on Amazon or BookBub to receive a new release alert!

CHASING SECRETS

ALYSSA RICHARDS

Ebook ISBN-13: 978-0-9991555-6-1
Paperback ISBN-13: 978-09991555-8-5
Editing by Peter Senftleben
Proofreading by 221b Baker St.

**Sign up for Alyssa's newsletter at to receive special offers and news
about her latest releases.**

You can follow her on:
Instagram

Contact Alyssa at:
authoralyssarichards@protonmail.com

For Lisa

"It is the stars. The stars above us, govern our conditions."
WILLIAM SHAKESPEARE

1

———

"You're lying." Barbara narrowed her eyes at her husband.

David raised his glass of champagne and broadcast his perfectly white, nearly electric smile that could have won an election. "Everything's fine."

She raised an eyebrow to scold him; he was evading. "I didn't say things weren't fine. I said you were lying."

He cleared his throat and gestured with his glass. "To our second anniversary, to yet another clean health report, and to the baby we weren't supposed to conceive."

He placed his hand over his jacket pocket. It was an unconscious move. She knew that's where he kept a photo of himself at the age of eight, his head resting across his mother's chest, her head wrapped in a colorful scarf, her skin pale and drawn against the white sheets of the hospital bed.

Barbara survived the cancer, his mother hadn't.

She ran her hand through her hair, grateful to have hair again. Grateful that it came in twice as thick as she once had, grateful that it didn't come back gray as she had been told that it might.

The ring of their champagne toast sounded clear in the quiet outdoor restaurant. She took only a tiny sip. A few cars drove by slowly, their engines relatively soft. A man whizzed by, standing on an electric-powered scooter, which hummed like the motor of a sewing machine.

David kissed her hand.

She studied his assuring smile and his soft expression. He was full of love and secrets. She never could read him clearly when his lips were on her skin or when he smiled at her in that way. In fact, she couldn't read him well at all. Not in the way she read other people.

"I saw another stack of medical bills come in this week," she said.

He looked at her hand and gave it a squeeze. "I'm making all the money we'll ever need to overcome whatever life throws at us. Don't you worry."

"I don't know how you do it." She cast him her most scrutinizing stare, the one she planned to use when their child was a teenager.

"I can do anything, when it comes to you." David tucked his napkin in his lap, his smile widening like he was pleased with himself. "And as far as not being able to read me the way you want, you're just going to have to trust me instead."

"I'd rather be able to read you." She arched her eyebrow again.

She'd never been able to figure out that little glitch with her talent. With anyone else, she got a gut feeling and would know quite a bit about that person. It was a skill she really appreciated because, oddly enough, she didn't trust people all that much otherwise.

When she realized she couldn't read David, her first

instinct had been to stay away from him. But she fell in love with him. She couldn't help herself. He treated her like a queen, never gave her any reason not to trust him.

Problem was, the more she overrode her instincts so that she could trust her husband, the less she trusted herself.

"One day soon I'll tell you why," he said.

"You know why I can't read you?" she asked.

"I have a theory." David sipped his champagne, kept his eyes on hers, like he was prepared for her question. Knew what she was going to ask and when. Everything he did was deliberate and full of care.

"Then tell me, because this has been driving me nuts for years."

"I will," he said. "Soon."

"Now. Please."

David was a planner. He always had a plan A and a plan B. Sometimes a plan C. Always thinking ahead. "Soon enough."

"Fine. Then you should know that I've been hiding something, too."

"You're not capable of keeping secrets from me."

"Actually, I am."

"Are you feeling okay? Is the baby alright?"

She pressed her hand to her still-flat stomach. "We're fine. Perfectly fine."

He gave a little exhale. "You're carrying my heart, you know. Our heart, actually."

She smiled and nodded. "I know."

"I've been thinking about something..."

"Wait, David, what I have to say is really important." She heard a whine in her voice she hadn't expected. He had spoiled her over the years and now she whined. She would have to break herself of that.

"Just real quick. Then I want to hear your secret. Okay?"

She wanted his undivided attention later, so she cleared her throat to make sure the whine was gone. "Fine. Shoot."

"Does the name Elias mean anything to you?"

"Elias...Elias..." Barb repeated the name in her mind and felt a swell of guilt in her chest. She wasn't supposed to know their baby's gender, yet. But the nurse had slipped and told her during the last ultrasound. David would flip when he found out they were having a girl if he was already thinking of boys' names. "No, I don't think so. Why do you want to know?"

"He works with one of my customers. I think there's something off about him."

She and David often discussed their impressions of other people, especially when they didn't know them that well. People had tells, signs they unwittingly shared that gave insight into who they were. Barbara picked up on those little signs better than most. She had a bizarrely keen radar when it came to reading people. It was probably genetic, her dad was the same way.

That knack had always come in handy. In college she could tell which boys were genuine and which ones were looking for meaningless hookups. Within a few moments of meeting new sorority sisters she knew who would be a loyal friend, and who wouldn't be trustworthy.

David had good instincts about people, too, but hers were better.

She couldn't remember anyone named Elias. "Why would you think I know him? Did he ask about me?"

"No, but my customer warned me that he has a history of making moves on other men's wives. Friendly and non-threatening at first, then crossing the line from professional to inappropriate. Seems he might be a little...unbalanced. I got the sense he could be dangerous." Intensity flashed in David's eyes, just for a moment.

She recognized the sign. It was an unconscious thing he did when he wasn't comfortable with what he was saying. Some people rubbed their nose when they weren't telling the truth. Others spoke rapidly, blinked too much or even broke into a sweat. For David, his eyes flared. Just slightly.

Deliberately, she'd never told him that he did this, it was one of the very few tells he had.

She exhaled hard to help clear her mind and focused on the cars that drove by as a distraction. Barbara didn't believe David's story about Elias. But she knew David was warning her off of him for a reason. Probably something more serious than he wanted to share. He was always protecting her.

"Then you need to stay away from him as well," she said. "Keep him away from your business."

He raised his glass of champagne. "I will. Another toast. Then I want to hear your secret. To your continued good health. And a wish on this, our second anniversary: May our next fifty years of marriage be as wonderful as our first two."

"And a lot healthier."

"They will be." He pressed his hand against the breast pocket of his blazer again. "I'll make sure of it." Their glasses clinked in a toast. "Now that you're healthy, I want to reopen the conversation about shutting the business down for a while so we can travel. We need to see the world while we can, just like we always wanted."

"Oh, David." They had talked about traveling the world together almost from their first date. But now that her mother had passed and her father had had his second heart attack, things had changed. "I can't leave Pop alone for that long. You know he depends on me."

"Then we'll plan a long vacation, to celebrate your recovery. Just a few months. I'll explain it all to you once we're away, but it's important." His eyes were wide and intense. His hands were tucked into tight fists on the table, the skin stretched taut over his white knuckles.

"A few months, David, that's—does this have something to do with that Elias person you just told me about?"

The brown sedan that drove toward them slowed down enough to catch her attention. The driver wore a trucker's hat and aviator sunglasses, and he stared straight at them.

"David—" She pointed to the driver. At the last second, he raised his arm level and straight and pointed a gun at them.

David turned, then quickly stood to hover over her.

"I love you, Barb! Go to the—" David's words were cut short by several loud pops. Blood spattered across her face and covered her glasses. Her husband's body jerked violently, then fell to the ground.

"NO!" she screamed.

Restaurant guests shrieked, dishes crashed.

Searing pain ripped through her shoulder and knocked her to the floor. Barbara crawled beneath the table, yanked her husband's arm and tried to pull him to her.

But he was heavy, unmoving.

Blood poured from the back of his head, his eyes wide open and unseeing.

S tars.

Everywhere.

Propped on the mantel, hung on the walls, patterned into the bath mats, painted on their dinnerware. One evening last year, after too many margaritas, she decided to count them. One hundred twelve was the final number at the time. But then David bought a few new ones, so she was no longer sure of the total.

Barbara Silver stretched out in her home that had once been overflowing with dreams coming true. Now haunted by living nightmares, she spent most nights in the recliner in the downstairs den, reading her cryptogram books, solving the endless puzzles. David used to buy her a fresh supply of these challenging puzzle books every month or so. He said he loved her nerdy addiction, that she was the perfect balance of beauty and brains.

When she had worked as many of the cryptograms as she could, she flipped through the travel-wish books she had assembled long before David died. She had put them together before they were married even. Before life took too many wrong turns to count.

Taped magazine pictures of Greece, Italy and the French Rivera looked up at her, reminding her of all the things she hadn't yet accomplished, of all the dreams that were still hanging on the vine.

Earlier that evening she had promised herself that she was going to sleep in the bed again. Kris, her sister-in-law, had said that buying a new bed was what she needed in order to sleep again. But even after the new bed arrived, she hadn't been able to sleep in it, or sleep anywhere at all.

In the eighteen months since David's death, the older condo's settling had begun to unnerve her. The creaks were loud enough that they woke her. They made her think David was still alive and walking the floor at night. Something he had been prone to doing in the last few months of his life. When she remembered that he was gone and she was alone, she worried that someone was creeping through her home. She had taken to checking the security alarm controls several times a night, making sure the two red lights were on.

She stared at the floodlight-covered tree branches that bent and dipped with the wind. The star-laden wind chimes that David had hung were over-performing and she threatened to take them down. Even though she knew she wouldn't. She wanted his beloved stars around her, those sparkling, heavenly reminders that she once had the promise of a truly bright future.

She had lost David and their child, along with her motivation to do most things. With the help of her father and sister-in-law, she had made it through the toughest part of the loss. But she couldn't get going on the redecorating. Many of the stars needed to come down, there were too many. And the bedroom they had started to outfit as a nursery needed to be redone.

Before lying down on most nights, she would open the door to the nursery to see the fifty or so glow-in-the-dark stars David had affixed to the ceiling. It was one of the last things he had done before he was killed.

"I love these, but the sheer number of stars in our home may have crossed us over into tacky," she'd said when she found him gluing them to the ceiling.

"It's not that many," he had said. "And they glow in the dark!"

When Barbara was little, she and her mother spent hours each week looking through the telescope. That's where she learned all about the constellations. When David learned about her love of stars, he became enthusiastic about them, too. Though she thought his interest had become an obsession.

"You have an odd fascination with stars," she said.

"One day soon I'll tell you why," he said. "Meanwhile, indulge me."

He never had the chance to tell her why he loved stars so much, or why she couldn't read him like she read other people or why he'd suddenly insisted that they had to travel the world.

Maybe her dad was right. Perhaps she needed to move altogether, work on creating new memories someplace else. Someplace without David's stars.

She counted one last time, then she knew she would have to stop. Eighteen. It had been eighteen months since David died, which meant that their baby would have been almost one year old by now. If she hadn't lost the baby on the day its father had been killed. Two deaths in one day.

The police had investigated the shooting and hadn't

been able to figure out who did it or why. She had given them the name Elias that David had mentioned. There was no trace of that name in David's client records and nothing in his files to indicate foul play. So they called his murder random. The shooting was just one of those things that happened in a cruel world, they had told her.

She checked the time: 3:33 a.m. She would have to pick up her father's prescriptions from the twenty-four-hour pharmacy on her way into work today. She made a mental note. Then she would go into the spa early, get her room ready for clients. While she gave her clients their facials, they would talk endlessly about their lives. That would give her a few hours' respite from thinking about hers.

A noise sounded above her, like a door opening. She squeezed her eyes shut, panic sprinted through her chest. She had never noticed noises in their home when David was alive. She wondered if it was his spirit that roamed the house, unsettled because he had never told her his secrets.

She looked quickly at the alarm keypad. Both red lights were illuminated which meant that she had remembered to turn the system on before lying down for the evening. Doors and windows were locked. She was fine. She filled her lungs with air and exhaled slowly, gently, to calm herself.

She wasn't going to call the police this time. Not again. Too many times they had come when she called in the middle of the night, too many times they inspected the house and they never found anyone. Once a policeman suggested she try therapy or antidepressants, so that she wouldn't hear noises in the middle of the night anymore. She almost clocked him upside the head with her shoe.

A creak whined into the quiet and fear propelled her upright and to the edge of the recliner. She switched off the lamp. She knew that particular sound. It was the spot in the middle of the second step on the stairway. Her heart pumped and kicked and begged her to run. She tiptoed across the den and into the kitchen, slid the largest knife from the wooden block and kept it at her side.

She stood with her back to the stove, her eyes shifting between the two doorways into the kitchen: one led from the small dining room, the other led from the den.

She listened hard in the quiet, expecting another sign that she had an intruder. The wind blew through the trees, forcing the outdoor chimes to dance their song. The house stayed quiet.

After a few moments she let out a deep breath, certain that she had lost her mind. No one else was here but her. She pointed the tip of the knife to the open slot on the wooden knife block, embarrassed that she had overreacted. Maybe she needed more therapy.

A long creak sounded and her stomach dropped hard and fast.

That was the last step on the staircase. She knew because that board had groaned since she and David walked through the house for the first time.

She watched each doorway for signs that someone was coming in, her head turning left, then right, left again. Until she felt like a sitting duck. If he had a gun, he would probably shoot her as soon as he saw her. She had to make a move.

Which way. Which way.

The back door had to be unlocked with a key, and those were hanging on the wall in the dark. It would be better to go out the front door. If he wasn't in the living room, he was probably in the den by now. She could get out the front door unnoticed.

She crouched low and peered around the corner,

watching the darkness for any movement. Step by quiet step she stuck close to the wall and moved toward the front door.

In her mind she practiced how quickly she would flip the two locks on the wooden front door. *One, two. One, two.* She hoped she had forgotten to lock the storm door. That lock was small and not easy to undo in the light of day, much less at night and under duress.

When she reached the living room, there was enough of a glow coming from the front porch light for her to see that no one else was in the space. Immediately she thought of all the shadowy places he could be. Beside the couch, behind the armchair.

She thought of making a run for it—just running fast through the room, and unlocking the doors as quickly as she could. The storm door would probably give way if she slammed it hard enough with her shoulder.

No. Quiet was better. Someone hiding in her home, probably spying on her, someone like that would want the upper hand. They would want her to panic.

Toe-heel, toe-heel, silent steps over the carpet. Her fast-running heart forcing her to draw in a breath through her mouth.

She reached the front door and unlocked the deadbolt.

Something clicked behind her and the stairway light came on, illuminating the foyer. Pain shot through her eyes from the bright light; she gasped. Knew right away that the click had been a gun.

"Drop the knife." His voice was low and his words were accented.

She released her grip and the knife clattered on the foyer tile. "Take whatever you want, just let me go."

"I'll let you go when you tell me where the diamonds

are. They're not at the warehouse. So, he must have hidden them here."

Diamonds? *The warehouse.* There had been four break-ins at David's warehouse since he died. "I don't know what you're talking about."

"Do you have a safe?"

"There's no safe."

"Then where are they? You're gonna give 'em back or I'm gonna do to you what I did to your husband. You got me?"

Her thoughts raced. Her husband. Diamonds. His murder hadn't been random. Elias. The name came back to her as if someone slid a notecard in front of her with his name printed in bright red ink.

"My husband didn't have any diamonds." Her voice pitched high with panic. "I don't know what you're talking about."

He pressed the gun to her head. "Your husband should have given them back when I gave him the chance." He grabbed both of her arms, pushed her onto the ground and tied her wrists with what sounded like duct tape. He was going to shoot her, she knew it.

"Elias, don't shoot!" she said quickly.

He loosened his grip, and the pressure of the gun drifted away.

"So, you do know what this is about," he said and pressed the gun flush against her head once again.

"I've called 911." Her voice was low, strong. She hoped he believed her. She hoped he wanted diamonds more than he wanted to hurt her.

He snatched her by the hair on the back of her head and turned her toward him. The only thing showing through his ski mask were his eyes—cold, brown, mean. His breath reeked of old cigarette smoke, rotting and wet.

"You return the diamonds and I'll leave you alone. If you don't, you know what will happen." He slammed her head against the tile floor and pain ricocheted inside her skull.

"I'll be back," he said. "Have the diamonds ready."

She laid there expecting him to step over her or shove her aside on his way out the front door. Instead, she heard him run up the stairs.

3

Barbara sat on the front steps of her neighbor's condo. She couldn't get the image of her intruder's eyes out of her head.

For the last eighteen months, two weeks and six days since his murder, she had yet to go one day without seeing her dead husband's sightless gaze staring up at her. Now she had another image to work out of her mind—those two brown eyes of the man who pointed a gun at her head tonight. The eyes that belonged to the man who murdered her husband.

"Did you recognize anything about him? Do you think he could have worked in David's warehouse?" Her neighbor, Terri, pulled her gray-streaked, shoulder-length dark hair into a ponytail holder. Then she wrapped a shawl around Barbara's bare arms.

Barbara ran her fingers over the tender lump that formed on the side of her head. "I've never seen him before."

"I just don't know how he would have gotten in. Not with the doors locked and the alarm on," Terri said.

"All I can think is that he must have come in through one of the upper story windows. Those aren't wired for the alarm system."

"How would he have gotten up there? Burglars don't usually travel with ladders when they're trying to break into a home." Terri waved to her own condo behind her, which was identical to Barbara's.

There were eighteen two-story condos in their small development. Six condos were attached to one another in three groupings. They were arranged in the shape of a square with one side missing, green space and a parking lot filling the middle area.

Most of the neighbors were older than Barbara, empty nesters who enjoyed their smaller homes and traveled to warmer climates in the winter. She and David had been only one of three young couples on the block.

Dark clouds rolled against the early morning sky, like pillows of black soot gliding over gray steel. The police car lights flashed with quiet alarm and reflected off of the condos that faced the parking lot. Many of her neighbors had come over and asked if she needed any help. Now they stood in small groups close to their own front steps, waiting for more information.

"Mrs. Silver?" A tall, slender man with wavy dark hair emerged from her home, two doors down. He didn't wear a uniform as the other policemen did. Instead he wore jeans and a long-sleeved shirt and a zippered jacket with the initials FBI across the back.

"She's over here!" Terri called.

Barb stood, wrapped her arms around herself, both to stem the early morning chill and to calm her nerves.

"Mrs. Silver, I'm Agent Hernandez. Charlotte FBI." His voice was strong, commanding, in control.

"Ms.," Barbara said. "Ms. Silver. My husband died a year and a half ago."

His lips thinned into a line. "I'm sorry."

She had heard more apologies in the past year than she had heard in her entire life. None of them fixed anything.

"Do you mind telling me what happened?" He rested his hands on his hips.

She told him how the guy with the ski mask was looking for diamonds and how she had no idea what he was talking about. She told him that he taped her wrists and then disappeared up the stairs again and that the alarm didn't go off until she opened the front door. "I don't know how he got in or out. But the upstairs windows aren't on the alarm system." She wondered if he was still hiding in the condo somewhere. Maybe in a corner of the attic. "When I finally managed to get out the front door, I ran to Terri's and kicked at her door until she answered. She cut the tape from my wrists and called you guys."

The agent looked at Terri. "You have the tape?"

"I have it inside," Terri gestured to her closed front door.

"Good. I'll have someone come over to get it into an evidence bag. Don't touch it again, we may be able to get some fingerprints."

Barbara knew what the agent was going to say next and she wanted to beat him to the punch. "Let me guess. There was no one inside."

"We didn't find anyone, ma'am," he said. "When your neighbor's 911 call came in, a friend of mine on the force asked me to help investigate. I've seen your call-in history."

Barbara rested her forehead in her hand.

"You had a break-in about a year and a half ago. And on eight separate occasions, you made 911 calls in the middle of the night—"

"You're not going to tell me I'm crazy, are you? Or that I need grief counseling? Because I've had a lot of therapy over the past year. Someone really did break into my home, tie me up and threaten me."

"If I were the kind of guy to say that to any woman, my wife would have served me with divorce papers." Agent Hernandez gave her a gentle smile that was intended to comfort.

Her shoulders relaxed a notch. She read his name tag: M. Hernandez.

From the way he spoke, she could tell that he had a methodical mind, he focused on facts and clues, he paid attention to every detail, no matter how small. Those details clearly paid off for him since he'd worked for the FBI. He obviously had a soft spot for women, liked taking care of them. But she worried that he wouldn't solve this case. Just like all the other police she'd spoken to over the last year and a half, she didn't think Agent Hernandez would find the man who killed her husband and who had threatened her tonight.

Her heart fell hard, like a heavy rock to the bottom of a lake. If the police couldn't help her, she had nowhere else to turn.

"We took some extra time to look around. I hope you don't mind."

"No. I don't mind." He was the first official in a long time to show her this kind of care and concern. "Did you find anything?"

"Come with me. I'll show you."

She hugged and thanked Terri for helping her. Then Barbara followed Agent Hernandez to the second story of her own home. Her body ached from too much anxiety and not enough sleep.

"It's just down here," he said.

They passed several uniformed policemen and women dusting for fingerprints and taking pictures of her home. Several of them nodded to her in a practiced way.

They walked down the long narrow hallway that she and David had painted yellow the week after they moved in. Then, up three carpeted stairs to the small bonus room that David had used as his office. After the break-in, every drawer in his desk had been yanked out and left on the floor, papers scattered everywhere. Now she knew what they had been searching for. What Elias had been searching for. But David didn't have any diamonds.

Agent Hernandez stood in the middle of the small room with the angled ceiling and turned to her. "How well do you know your neighbors?" He pointed to the far wall, the common wall her unit shared with the condo next door.

"Mr. Burke lived there when we first moved in. Older man, very friendly. He had two dogs and we chatted when he took them out for a walk."

"He's not there anymore?"

"No, he moved to Florida about a year and a half ago, I guess. Right before David was killed."

"Right *before* David was killed." He said and scribbled something on his notepad. "Do you know the new owners?" He widened his stance and crossed his arms. His words were smooth and intentional, like steel fishing hooks laid out as bait.

Barb shook her head. "Mr. Burke said the man made him an offer that was too good to turn down. He apologized before he left, saying that the new owner was young. Everyone in here has owned their condo for years. People were concerned it might be a college student. You know, loud music and parties and overgrown grass and so forth."

"Made him an offer?"

"Yeah, he didn't even have his unit on the market. But when the guy made the offer, Mr. Burke snapped it up." Her words slowed. "Are you saying the guy who broke in lives next door?"

"Just a second." He made a few more notes. "Have you ever seen the new owners?"

Barb ran her hands over her face; her teeth were starting to gnash against one another. Her husband's killer in her own home, the gun, the threats, the flurry of police in her house, and now this line of questioning—a slow-building scream was rising inside of her.

He raised his eyebrows at her, waiting for an answer.

"Well, there's a guy who comes in and out occasionally. Youngish. Late twenties, maybe. He keeps to himself. Always wears a baseball cap and these sort of sleek, sporty sunglasses. He doesn't speak. Just parks out front here, keeps his head down, goes right inside. If David were still around, I would have taken him a cake or a pie or something and welcomed him to the neighborhood. Tried to make friends. But I haven't really been in the mood for socializing this year." Her tone was peevish in spite of her intention to sound cooperative.

Agent Hernandez nodded, his blue eyes sharp and focused. "Do you know if he was here last night? Do you remember seeing his car?"

"He drives a dark blue Ford sedan. I don't have any idea if he was here or not."

Agent Hernandez put on a pair of purple latex gloves, the kind she had seen doctors and nurses wear. "Okay, after I show you this, I want you to leave your home for tonight. If you can swing it, it would be a good idea if you left town for a few weeks. Let this guy lose track of you. Let us focus on finding him. Do you have any out-of-town relatives you can stay with for a while? Might be safer that way."

Her heart banged against her ribs.

"At the very least, don't come back until this is sealed."

"Until what is sealed?"

He pointed to a small square door in the wall near the floor; the silver handle had splotches of black powder on it. He placed a finger over his lips and drew his gun. "Doors like this typically just lead to a crawl space. People usually leave them empty or use them for light storage. Builders leave them unfinished because it gives homeowners access to install exterior lighting and so forth. Have you ever been inside this area? Maybe you stored Christmas decorations or high school yearbooks in here at one time?"

"No," she said. "We never had much stuff."

He opened the small door a crack, then nudged it open all the way. He shined his flashlight with one hand, aimed his gun with the other. On the opposite side of the small space was a brown wall with a sizable hole punched through. On the other side of the hole was another storage space that mimicked hers, including the square outline of light around a small door.

"State code requires builders to put a firewall between all condos and apartments. Sometimes it's called a one-hour wall. If there were a fire in your neighbor's house, this wall would keep it from spreading to your home for at least an hour." He pointed to the hole. "Someone has knocked a pretty big hole through this firewall, big enough to crawl through. So, whoever lives next door could get inside your home—"

"Without me even knowing," she finished his sentence. "Without even setting off the alarm." Her chest clenched tight and her hands tingled.

Agent Hernandez closed the door. "You've had one break-in that you know about. There were numerous occasions when you thought you heard footsteps when you were here alone."

Her throat was painfully dry. "Several times a week."

"I think you've had more break-ins than you've known about and I think your neighbor is our prime suspect. You need to move your valuables and important papers out of your home."

Her entire body shook from the inside out as if she were deeply cold. David's killer lived next door and had been in the condo while she was there. "I don't have anything expensive. My engagement ring is the only diamond I own, and that's still in my top drawer. David said he kept all of our papers in the safety deposit box at the bank. I haven't looked there since he passed. I just—I just haven't done it." She'd run out of excuses as to why she still hadn't taken care of certain things. She just hadn't wanted to undo anything David had done—the stars, the chimes, even the safety deposit box. As if keeping those intact would keep him close to her.

Agent Hernandez put his hand on her shoulder and patted it twice. "After my first wife left, it took me a good two years before I got it together again. I know it doesn't seem like it now, but one day you'll find your fresh start. Just trust your instincts."

She stuffed her hands into the front pockets of her baggy sweatshirt. She had always trusted her instincts, until David came into her life.

The agent pushed David's desk across the room until it was flush against the small door. "This won't keep him out. You need to get someone in here today to rebuild that firewall. If this were my home, I'd have the guy use concrete or brick to do the repair."

"My sister-in-law is in real estate. I'll ask her for a referral." She ran her hand through her hair and noticed her hand shaking. She didn't know if it was fear or rage.

"I'm going to write up my report. We should all be out of here in the next thirty minutes or so."

"Agent Hernandez?" she asked.

"Yes, ma'am?"

"Would you wait here while I throw a few things in a bag? I'm going to leave when you leave."

"I think that's wise."

IF IT HADN'T BEEN clear to her before, it was all too apparent to her now. She had to move. David was gone, the life they had was long over. The family life she thought they were going to share within these walls was never going to happen. She pulled on a black t-shirt, lifted her suitcase from the closet shelf, and opened it on the bed.

The guy next door was likely the same one who was responsible for the earlier break-in, the same guy who broke into the warehouse and the same person who killed her husband.

The eyes of her husband's killer flashed in her mind. The meanness of them had left a mark, like an emotional tattoo. Diamonds, he had said. That had to be a mistake. David didn't have any diamonds. She grabbed a random assortment of clothes from her closet and dresser drawers until her arms were full, then she tossed them into the suitcase. She had no idea what, exactly, she was packing. She didn't care; whatever she ended up with she'd make it work. She just wanted out.

She opened a small drawer in her bedside table and took out the gun her father had bought for her years ago. It wasn't loaded, she'd never used it. She would have to start carrying this now.

She went into the bathroom, took her makeup travel case from beneath the sink and began filling it. She heard Agent Hernandez on his phone in the hallway telling someone at the police station what he had found. The more detail he relayed as to what he had seen in her condo, the angrier she became.

She yanked the shallow makeup drawer from beneath the counter and emptied the contents into the unzipped case. She noticed the small envelope taped to the underside of the drawer.

David had asked her to keep the safety deposit box key somewhere safe, someplace where no one else would find it. "Even if someone broke in," he had said. He held her hands. "If something happens to me, you remember to go there and get all of our papers and things."

She'd told him to stop being morbid. A chill shimmied through her body. Now she realized. He must have known someone would come looking.

Without I.D. she didn't think anyone could get to their safety deposit box, even if they had the key. But there were fake I.D.s. Good ones. People's identities were stolen all the time. Apparently, David knew that and didn't want to take any chances.

She ripped the envelope from the underside of the drawer and opened its fastener. The shiny silver key was still inside. She closed the envelope again and pushed it into the very bottom of her front jeans pocket. She would go by the bank as soon as they opened. The idea that she might find a pouch full of diamonds left her feeling sick.

Once outside, Agent Hernandez ripped off a page from his pad and handed it to her. "That's your case number at the top of the form. They'd like for you to come by the station tomorrow so they can ask you some additional questions. One of the detectives may want to question you again."

She thanked him and pulled the house keys from her purse and locked the front door. The star key chain that David had given her swung from the lock. "Not that this will do any good if Elias wants to get in."

Agent Hernandez stopped short. "Who's Elias?"

She quickly told him how David had mentioned that name to her on the night he was killed. She also told him how she called the intruder Elias and how he responded. "He didn't admit it, but I think that's his name."

"He's a client of your husband's business?"

"David had said it was someone who worked with one of his clients. I told the police all of this right after David was killed. I checked the warehouse client records and couldn't find that name."

"I'd like to look into that a little further if you don't mind. I have your cell phone listed as your main contact number. Is that the best number for you?"

She opened the trunk to her car and put her suitcase and carryon inside. "Yes." She sighed, turned to face Agent Hernandez and caught sight of the front of her townhome. She remembered holding David's hand when they walked up those brick steps for the first time. While the realtor removed the key from the lockbox, she and David shared a quiet kiss. "This is the one," she'd said. "This is going to be our new home. I can feel it." She'd grinned so wide it had made her cheek muscles hurt.

"Barbara?" Agent Hernandez asked.

She shook her head to clear the memory. Blue lights flashed across her once loving home.

"Yes. Sorry. My cell phone is the best number."

A blue sedan drove slowly on the street in front of the complex. She leaned to the side to get a better look, and froze.

"What's the matter?" he asked.

"That blue car on the street. I think that's him. The guy from next door."

Agent Hernandez put his hand on his gun and started across the parking lot. Before he reached the halfway mark, the blue Ford revved its engine.

"Stop!" he yelled. "Police!"

But the car didn't stop, and its tires squealed.

4

——————

Barbara sipped on the double shot of Bailey's, tugged the soft plaid blanket over one shoulder and sank lower into her father's worn leather recliner. Her childhood home looked just as it did when she and her brother lived there as children, and when their mother was still alive. Barbara was diligent about maintaining all of her mother's homemaking touches—green ferns hanging on the front porch, fresh flowers on the breakfast table and her father's favorite cornbread on Sundays.

"I'm sure you don't have any idea what diamonds he's talking about," her father said for the third time since she had told him her story.

"No, I don't." She studied him. His thick gray hair was combed straight back, proof that he had taken a hot bath earlier. She had called him before he turned in and he'd told her that he had taken Miller, his beloved German shepherd, on his evening walk, as was a part of his continued recovery therapy.

"Exercise and diet," the cardiologist had told her father.

"Those are your game-changers." Barbara reminded her father of this often. In turn her father often reported in when he complied. That was the nature of their relationship these days.

When her mother died Barbara began checking in on him daily. Then he had his first heart attack, and she took care of getting his prescriptions filled. When he had his second heart attack, she continued all of those things and began keeping an eye on his nutrition to make sure he ate well. David used to joke that he played second fiddle to his father-in-law.

Her father's dark blue eyes narrowed, he was working his way through the problem. A former sergeant in the army and a retired police officer, he was accustomed to solving mysteries. When she told him about the hole in the firewall, he told her what she already knew, that she couldn't go back there. Not even after the firewall was fixed. Though the sun wasn't up yet, he texted his daughter-in-law, Kris, and told her to list the property immediately.

"When the guy first said that he was looking for diamonds, I thought—this is some kind of mistaken identity. He's got the wrong house and the wrong person and I'm going to get shot because of something somebody else did. But then he talked about how, if I didn't turn them over, that I was going to die like my husband did. So, he knew David. And he definitely recognized the name Elias."

"Diamonds," her father said. "Just doesn't sound like David. He was a straight arrow, that one. Treated you well."

"Like a queen." She thought about how David had insulated her, taken care of everything for her, hardly let her lift a finger. She'd grown comfortable with that, so much so that she had stopped making some of her own choices.

The Irish whiskey warmed her from the inside out, she closed her eyes. Different images flashed in a chaotic order —David quizzing her on the names of different types of stars, gluing stars to the ceiling in the nursery, kissing her belly, Agent Manny Hernandez opening the small storage door and showing her the hole in the firewall, her neighbor speeding down the road with his tires squealing. "Elias," she heard David say at the outdoor restaurant. The man in the trucker's hat and the aviator sunglasses driving down the street in the brown sedan, his arm lifting toward them with the gun in his hand. The man in the ski mask who held a gun at her head.

Her glass hit the carpet with a thud and she jerked upright.

"You okay?" her father asked.

She nodded. Rubbed her eyes and picked up the glass. "Do you think we could have missed the name Elias somewhere in David's records?"

"I'll go back to the warehouse in the morning and search again. You stay here with Miller." The dog sat upright and her dad patted his head. "I've taught you how to protect yourself. You need to start carrying that gun I bought for you."

"It's in my purse," she said. "I need to go by the bank in the morning." She felt the outline of the silver safety deposit box key in her pocket. "The FBI agent suggested I get out of town for a while. Give them a chance to find this guy without my being in harm's way."

She watched her father's jaw muscle work and she knew he didn't like the idea.

"For how long?" he asked.

"I don't know. He said it might be safer if I were out of

sight. I'm thinking it might be safer for you, too, if I weren't around. I don't want this guy figuring out where you or Kris live. What do you think?"

He drew in a deep breath, exhaled hard. "Well, I hate the idea of this guy running you out of town. Where would you go?"

She felt his heart ache. They had always been close, but since her mother's death their relationship had become even closer. "Maybe it's not a good idea."

"I don't guess I could tuck you away in the backyard...set up a tent like when you were a little girl? When you pretended to travel someplace exotic?"

Her lips curved into a smile at the memory—seeing her mother standing on the other side of the kitchen window, watching her brother run around the tent with his Nerf guns, listening to her father yell from the side yard that Stephen needed to leave her alone. She thought of her own condo and all the happy times she and David had shared there. A vision of David's dark brown coffin being lowered into the ground came to mind, the smell of fresh earth and white flowers came with it. Then she saw the flashing blue police lights across her front door from earlier this morning, the smile slid from her face until it was completely gone.

Her father leaned back and narrowed his eyes as if he read her mind. "You'll find a new home." That hadn't been the first time he'd given her that suggestion. He glanced around the room and sighed. Like he relived memories of his own. "Might be good for you to have a fresh start, anyway. Sometimes memories don't do you any favors. They're strong as steel and they can make you their prisoner."

She followed her father's line of sight, landing finally on the wall of family photos that highlighted her and her brother Stephen's early school years, her wedding, Stephen's wedding, and an 8x10 of her mother in the middle of it all. It was at that moment she realized most of her life was actually in the past. For the last year and a half, she hadn't been living. She had only been reliving.

5

Cara, the banker, was startlingly young. Her jet black hair was slicked high in a twist, and large flat freckles coated her nose and cheeks. Her black suit was boxy with shiny gold buttons down the front, and on-trend shoulder pads that were, according to the magazines, making a comeback. Unfortunately the sharp angles brought attention to the fact that the jacket was far too big for her. The overall combination made her look as if she were a kid playing dress-up in her mother's business suit. Barb wanted to give her some advice. She wanted to tell her that ideals were a bad investment.

The banker compared Barbara's driver's license to something on her computer screen. "Oh. Here you are. You should have told me you shared this box with your husband." She smiled a pageant-worthy smile and emphasized the word husband, as if Barb's marital status entitled her to a higher rank within the bank's system.

"He's deceased." Barbara produced the death certificate from her purse.

The banker winced like she'd bitten her tongue. She

carefully avoided eye contact with Barbara and accepted the certificate with an apologetic nod. She stared at the screen and tapped on her computer keyboard. "I'll make a note on your account."

"I'd like to take his name off of our account and our checks, too, please." Barbara knew she ought to have done this over a year ago, but she hadn't been able to find the strength.

Cara said she would. She made a handwritten note for herself and led Barbara to a small room lined with four walls of silver safety deposit boxes. A room full of secrets.

"This one is yours. Here." Cara pointed to the medium-sized box, her trendy taupe-colored nails shiny under the canned lighting. Barbara imagined her flipping through endless magazines to find just the right color. As if the right image could create the perfect life. Cara put her key with the orange fob into the lock.

Barb stared, waiting.

"Now you just put your key in that chamber right there." Cara's tone was sweet and coaxing.

Barb inserted her key. She'd never had a safety deposit box, never saw the reason for it. David was the one who insisted they have one. He took care of maintaining it.

Cara pulled the long box and placed it on the table that had privacy panels on three sides. "Take as long as you need to. I'm just at my desk if you need help with anything."

Barbara watched after her until she was gone. She lowered herself onto the cold plastic chair and placed her hands on the metal box. David had been the last person to put anything inside. She was visiting with a ghost.

There couldn't be diamonds inside. Wouldn't be, she assured herself. David never stole anything, ever. He paid their taxes in full and on time, tipped generously, gave to charity, lived well beneath his means. He was as honest and down-to-earth as they came. He even worked as a park ranger while he was in college in New York. He loved helping people. He wasn't someone who stole diamonds.

She lifted the lid without a noise.

Inside were the standard items she had expected to see: the deed to their condo, his passport and hers, their wills, birth certificates, and their marriage certificate. There was two thousand dollars in cash, because David had been convinced that there would be a banking crisis at some point, and he wanted immediate access to cash. She put the documents and the cash into the center section of her purse and zipped it shut. She stared into the empty box.

No diamonds.

Maybe David's death was as the police had said, tragic and random. The guy who had broken in could have gotten the wrong house. The wrong person. David hadn't stolen any diamonds. But maybe someone who worked for David did. She would tell Agent Hernandez to look into the employees again.

She stepped out of the small room. "I'm finished," she said. "I left the box on the table."

Cara's expression was wary. "Ms. Silver?"

"Yes?"

"I found another account under your husband's name. A safety deposit box. It's in his name only." Cara pointed to the computer screen that Barb couldn't see.

Barbara's throat was dry and she forced a swallow. "Oh. Right. I forgot about that one." David had never mentioned another safety deposit box.

"If you have his will that shows you inherit his property, I can give you the key."

"Thank you for reminding me. Gosh, I almost walked

right out of here without it." She unzipped her purse, removed the will and hoped Cara didn't see her hand shaking.

"I have our marriage certificate, too, if you need it. What's his is mine." Including the trouble, she thought.

The banker gave her a cursory smile, one that said she knew Barb's husband had kept the safety deposit box a secret. She examined the will, and when she was done she said, "Okay, looks like everything is in order. It's box 397, a bigger one this time."

"Yes, I remember." Her teeth ground against one another. Suddenly she needed to know how much monthly rent David had paid for a large box. How dare he spend their money without discussing it with her?

After the banker handed her the box, she left her alone as before. Silence, except for her quick, angry breaths. She stared at the box, wishing it would disappear. It wasn't the monthly rent that concerned her. She was terrified of what David might have hidden inside.

She squeezed her eyes shut for a long second, conjuring strength. She opened the lid. Inside was a thick white envelope, unsealed. There was also a Star of David keychain made of iron, with a small bronze key attached. She turned the cool metal over in her hand. David had rattled on endlessly about different types of stars, their meanings and origins. He had even quizzed her on them. He made sure she knew the answers to his questions. But he never mentioned an extra safety deposit box or that he had hidden a key. Fury burned in her gut and its flames licked at her heart. She should have stayed away from David when she first realized she couldn't read him. Now he kept her on the outside, even in death.

Maybe he did take those diamonds.

She removed the key that had opened the safety deposit box in front of her and held it up to the key attached to the Star of David. They were identical in size and shape. Different in color. Could it have been a post office box key? No. The two keys were so similar. It had to fit yet another safety deposit box.

She looked inside the 9x12 envelope, half expecting, half dreading that she would see jewels. Instead she found two passports and two drivers' licenses. She put them on the table. One passport and driver's license had David's face, albeit with a lighter hair color and glasses. David didn't wear glasses. She squinted at the name: Richard Wilson.

Her body went limp.

Had this was what David had been referring to at their last dinner together? That she would find out soon enough why she couldn't get a read on him? Was he planning to tell her that his real name was Richard Wilson?

She traced her index finger along the edge of David's likeness. "Who are you?" she whispered.

She opened the second passport and startled at the sight of her own photo. The name read Mara Wilson. The second license was the same as the passport—her photo with the name Mara Wilson. She scooted away from the table, stared at the fake licenses and passports.

He had pushed her for years to travel, saying that they needed to see the world while they were young. But that must not have been about travel at all. He must have actually needed to escape. He would have taken his pregnant wife on the run and he obviously wasn't planning for them to come back. She crumpled the white envelope in her fist. David must have stolen diamonds from someone after all.

She took the key with the Star of David keychain to the

banker who was still sitting at her desk outside the front door.

"Excuse me." Barb noticed the edge to her voice. "Can you tell me which box this key belongs to?"

Cara examined the key. "This looks like it would fit a safety deposit box, but I don't think this is one that belongs to our bank. Ours are all silver. Let me check the account list again to see if your husband had another box besides the two we already know about." Her fingers flew over the keys and she scanned the large screen.

After a long while, she shook her head. "I don't see any other accounts listed here either for you and your husband or for your husband alone. You might try some of the other banks in town. As long as you have his will and the other certificates, they ought to give you access." Cara tilted her head to the side and managed a weak, sympathetic smile. "Sorry. Good luck."

Barb took the keychain and shoved it into her purse.

Once in the parking lot, she dialed her sister-in-law, Kris, who started talking from the moment she answered and before Barb could say anything.

"Oh, honey. I spoke to Pop, then I went out to your condo first thing this morning. Bless your heart. Diamonds? That's not possible. Did you get my messages?"

"I've been at the bank, so I had my phone turned off. Thanks for going out there." She pressed her hand against her forehead and told Kris about the passports and licenses she had found in David's safety deposit box.

"He was obviously planning for us to take on different identities, to leave town. Forever, I guess. And leave Pop? Leave my family? He knew I would never have wanted that."

"Are you sure? I mean, of course you're sure. I just can't believe—David was so good to you."

She felt the scream building again. David's secret life, the break-ins, the man with the gun, the diamonds, fake passports. All of it was taking a toll. She was rattled. "I don't think I knew him as well as I thought I did."

"Have you told Pop about the passports?" Kris asked.

She lowered the window and drew in a deep breath of fresh air for clarity, for strength. "He's had two heart attacks, I really don't want to tell him something that gives him his third."

"He'll be twice as upset if he hears the story from someone else. And you know he's going to make someone at the station give him the details if you don't."

Kris was right. She would have to tell him.

Computer keys clacked in the background. "There. Your condo is officially listed."

"Thanks." The thought hit her. The happy home she'd thought she had with David hadn't even been real. Because she never truly knew him. A flash of the hole in the firewall came back to her and she shivered. "I don't want to go back there."

"I don't blame you. Why don't I go ahead and hire movers? We'll put your stuff in storage and you could stay with me until you find your next place."

"I'll take you up on the movers and the storage. But you're almost eight months pregnant, Kris, and Stephen is on duty overseas. If this guy is watching me, I shouldn't be seen going in and out of your house. I couldn't put you in danger like that."

Kris was quiet. If she hadn't been pregnant, Barb knew she would have told her to come on over. That she had an alarm system and several of Stephen's guns in the house. But now that she had a baby on the way, her thought processes had changed. Barb understood.

"There was an FBI agent at the house last night. He suggested I get out of town for a while. You know, get off this guy's radar. I've got some vacation time saved up, so I'm thinking about it."

"If you decide to go, I'll watch over Pop while you're gone," Kris said.

"You're supposed to be resting, right? Last thing you need right now is to care for someone else. Especially Pop, he can be a lot of work."

"I'm not on bed rest. Just extra rest. Focusing on him will keep me from worrying about what kind of mother I'm going to be. Last night I had a dream that I put the baby down somewhere and couldn't remember where. Besides, you know there's no way Pop would tolerate anyone but me."

Barb smiled at her sister-in-law's dream. When she was pregnant she'd read about the stress dreams that pregnant women could have. And she knew Kris was right about Pop.

"Oh, you know? I have this client who's renting out his mountain house in Brevard. It's not a lot of space, but it would be great for you. Very remote, it's on a lake, right near one of the waterfalls. He says you can actually hear the falls when the house is quiet."

Barbara started the car and looked around the parking lot to see if anyone was watching her. She didn't see the man she would have recognized as her neighbor. "Alright, that sounds good."

"Great, I'll let him know. There's a management company up there that takes care of the place. Really, it's just one woman, Lillian Grossman. She's a talker and I think she'll probably mother you to pieces, which might not be a bad thing right now. I'll call her and let her know you're coming. She also has this very small spa just off the main square in the downtown area. Maybe you could pick up a few shifts while you're up there? That way you're not sitting around and worrying too much."

Barbara slipped her sunglasses on and pulled into traffic. She definitely didn't want to sit around anymore. "Some work would be nice." Her call waiting beeped and she glanced at the screen. It wasn't a number she recognized. Robocall, probably. She sent it to voicemail.

"I'll call Lillian and rent the home under my name, so there's no trace to you. Not that anyone would be looking at my records to find you. But still. Better safe than sorry," Kris said.

"Right. Good point." She listened to Kris typing for a minute, then said, "I found this key in David's safety deposit box."

"What kind of key?"

"I think it fits another safety deposit box, but I don't have any paperwork on it. Do you have any idea how I would figure out which bank it belongs to?"

"You would just have to go from bank to bank and show your I.D. and all your...certificates and things and see if David had an account there."

She knew Kris avoided saying death certificate and she wondered how long it would take before people stopped tiptoeing around her. She figured it might be sooner now that David's secrets were coming to light.

"That's what I thought." She checked her rearview mirror for any signs of her neighbor.

After a long pause, Kris said, "Alright. Now, I've got it all under control. The repairs, everything."

She knew that Kris did, too. The woman could whip details into a straight line like nobody's business. Kris and Pop were spoiling her, and had been for over a year and a half now. Her father had taken over the management of what was left of David's business. Her sister-in-law had kept her upright emotionally with the patience and care of a saint.

Her voicemail alert sounded. "Thanks, Kris. I appreciate this more than you realize."

As soon as she said her good-byes with her sister-in-law, Barbara wondered if she was overreacting. Maybe it would have sent a stronger message if she stayed in town, went to work as usual. She shouldn't be bullied out of her own hometown.

She clicked the voicemail icon to play the message in case it was a client trying to get on her calendar.

"Hello, Barbara." His voice was low and smooth

Terror shot through her every nerve ending. She could almost smell the stale cigarette breath coming through the phone.

"I just wanted to check in to see how your search is going. I have high hopes for you, doll. You're going to come through for me, aren't you? You'll make your husband's mistakes right. Remember, I'm never far away. I'm going to keep a close eye on you."

She swerved off the busy road, her heart drumming so fast it skipped beats. Her hands shook. She dug through her purse for the card that Agent Hernandez had given her.

She held it up so she could see the numbers clearly, then forwarded the voicemail to the number on the card. She dialed his number and left a message telling him about the call. The white hood of her Honda gleamed brightly in the sun and she realized that the guy who held her at gunpoint, whatever his name was, would know her car.

6

B arb downshifted her father's old Jeep into third gear to climb the mountainside road. The car engine growled low and deep, chugged around the steep curves and gravel-covered road. The Star of David keychain she'd found in David's safety deposit box banged against her kneecap, a nagging reminder of what she still had to figure out. Her father's night vision binoculars slipped off of the dash and landed between the two seats where she kept her gun.

Her father finally, reluctantly, agreed with her that she ought to get out of town for a while. But not before he insisted she take his Jeep and carry her gun and call him every day. He also held her hands, looked her in the eye and told her that he couldn't lose her, too. He had lost his wife, and his son had been deployed to the Middle East, so she had to stay safe.

"Use those good senses you have, sweetheart."

She promised she would.

Silver guardrails were only along certain road edges that looked more like cliffs than mountain slopes. Twisted strands of metal stood testament to some kind of nasty accident. The remaining road sections had no safety rails at all.

Even though hers was the only car on the road, she kept her speed under forty miles per hour. The more dramatic the incline, the lower the red needle dipped to the left on the speedometer. There was barely any margin on either side of the road for what few guardrails they did have. She took note of the fact that there weren't any streetlights.

When she arrived at the Pisgah National Forest, the ranger stopped her at the gate and checked the paperwork Kris had sent her. He looked to be in his late sixties with his white hair and mustache and rounded belly. He took a black pen from his pocket and wrote something on the front page of the stapled sheets of paper.

She studied his brown uniform and remembered how David had told her that he left the park ranger service in New York before they had met. He had decided that there wasn't enough money in his first career choice. So, he got into import/export. That had to have been his motivation for stealing the diamonds, she decided—money.

"These gates close at seven p.m. to the public. They won't open again until nine the next morning. You can drive in and out with this access code I've written down, but I'll warn you that the system can be unpredictable. The gates are old. Sometimes they don't work. The few folks that live back in here usually just stay in at night. Otherwise you would have to park here in the public lot and walk to your house and that's going to be about three miles for you. Now, that's not that far, but at night and with the wildlife we have out here, it's not safe." He handed the paperwork back to her and raised one of his white eyebrows in a warning.

She thanked him for the advice and confirmed the directions to the house. They didn't sound too difficult which was a good thing, because the directional app on her new phone only showed her driving along nameless roads. The cell signal dropped to one bar. She was officially off the grid.

She didn't at all mind that she had to be in by seven. The whole point of being up here was to lie low and be out of sight until the police caught her former neighbor. This location certainly fit. But the idea of the gate being locked behind her in a few hours left her feeling captive.

The dirt path was narrow, only wide enough for one small car, or half of a larger one. Two of the Jeep's tires rolled through the brush. Kris had told her that there were only a handful of houses throughout the entire preserve, and that she would have to search for hers—#105 Pine Ridge Road.

She kept the Jeep in low gear, looking through the dense, dark forest for signs of something residential—a driveway, a mailbox, a clearing. Small bits of sunlight dropped to the darkened floor like splotches of luminescent paint. The road's curves became increasingly sharp and twisted, guiding her deep into the thick woods. There was no more than a few feet of straightaway before the road turned again. And again. She understood now why the park ranger said that the few residents who lived up here didn't leave at night.

When she rounded the next turn, she slammed on the brakes, drew in a sharp breath. The black bear in the middle of the road stood on its hind legs and roared so loud her bones shook. Three cubs ran at the mother's feet. The bear growled again, like a scream, her mouth wide, full of teeth and rage.

Trees hemmed Barb in on either side, there wasn't enough room on the road to turn the Jeep around. If the bear didn't go away, she had no choice but to hit the gas and plow forward. Fury rose inside of her like hot lava, erupted against the inside of her skull and threatened to overflow. Her hands gripped the steering wheel. She revved the engine, the only growl she had.

They stared at each other for a long moment, then the mother bear stepped toward the Jeep. Barb opened her mouth, her teeth bared, and a long, angry scream built slowly, came from somewhere deep inside. It rattled from her soul, fueled by shattered dreams, and shook something loose from within. It was her grief, up and out, riding on a guttural cry that echoed into the forest.

The three cubs tumbled over one another, scurrying by their mother's legs, and scampered into the woods. The mother roared again, fell to all fours and lumbered after them, never once taking her eyes off of Barb.

They ambled out of sight. Barb gasped for air.

Then the tears fell unexpectedly. Her sobs were loud, rising from the layers of fear.

Questions. So many—old ones, new ones, all persistent and endlessly nagging. Who was David, really? Why had he stolen diamonds? Where would he have even gotten them and where were they now? Would the police stop Elias before he found her? Would Elias go after Kris or her father? And why hadn't she been able read David? She grabbed a stack of fast food napkins from the passenger seat and wiped the dark streams of mascara from her face. She lowered her window by half, drew in deep inhales of fresh pine and mountain air.

A powerful rush of water in the distance, the call of a hawk from overhead. Humans were an afterthought in the preserve.

She drove onward through the woods. Half of a lone black mailbox stuck out from an overgrown bush. The number 105 was pasted across the top. She checked the address Kris had given her: 105 Pine Ridge Road. She turned from the dirt road and gunned the Jeep to climb the gravel drive, rocks grinding and popping beneath her tires.

A man burst through the line of bushes and her heart jackknifed into her throat. She slammed on the brakes, his hands splayed on the hood of the Jeep.

He was tall and muscular with straight dark hair visible beneath his brimmed hat. She searched the shape of his face, his head, tried to imagine what he would look like in a baseball cap and different sunglasses.

He walked toward her driver's side door. She put the Jeep into reverse and backed away. He stopped, laughed, and raised both hands in the air as if he surrendered. "Sorry! Sorry. I live next door, I'm Griffin." He pointed to a house that was mostly closeted by the trees, the apex of its broad front window the only part of the house that was visible.

Griffin...

She repeated his name in her mind again and again. Not Elias.

When she didn't say anything, he put his hands in his back pockets, kept his distance. "I didn't mean to startle you, I didn't think anyone was staying here."

She slid the gun from between the seats and tucked it into her back pocket. He didn't look like her former neighbor, but she couldn't be completely sure.

"Hey," she finally said and kept her hand on the gun.

"I'm sorry if I'm trespassing. I've been cutting through to catch that trail down there." He pointed to something behind her and she didn't turn around. "No one has been in this house for the last couple of months so I usually just make this my shortcut."

"Would you take off your glasses, please?" she asked and eased from the car.

"I'm sorry?"

"Your sunglasses. Would you take them off."

"Oh. Sure."

She tightened her grip on the gun handle and prepared to aim the barrel at him. If he had the brown eyes she had seen behind the ski mask the other night, she wouldn't hesitate to aim the gun at him point-blank. And if he charged her she would fire the gun the way her father had taught her when she was twelve. She wouldn't so much as tell him to stop or warn him that she was going to fire.

He removed his hat and glasses, an isolated stream of sunlight making the black in his hair shimmer. His light gray eyes made her relax, and also made her knees a little weak.

"Thanks." She released her hand from the gun and stepped around the open door of the Jeep.

"I hope I don't look like whoever it is you didn't want to see."

"No," she said. "You don't."

He looked at her with a half-smile for a moment then shook his head, as if he had forgotten his manners. "I didn't catch your name." He extended his hand cautiously.

Griffin, Griffin... She shook his hand.

"Barbara."

"Nice to meet you, Barbara."

His hand closed around hers, its warmth comforting. He looked smart. Brilliant, maybe. Doggedly determined with everything he did. His stance was wide and confident, and even though she had almost flattened him, he seemed unfazed. As if he dodged the dangerous and unexpected every day. He liked her, she knew. The signs were there.

There were flecks of distrust, uncertainty in those eyes the color of ice. He had loved too hard with that big heart of his, she suspected. Gotten left or trampled in the process. Still he showed up, open, trying. A thirst for life.

"Are you here on vacation?" he asked.

"Yeah. Love the mountains." She realized she had been quietly staring.

"Me, too. You picked a great spot. We have a lake out back, it's perfect for swimming, boating and fishing. Plenty of hiking trails around and we have over 250 waterfalls."

"Two hundred and fifty?"

"More waterfalls here than any other county in the country. I'd be happy to show you around."

She nodded before she knew she was even answering.

"Excellent. Do you hike?"

"Yeah, I do." She couldn't remember the last time she had taken a hike, but suddenly she was ready to reclaim that interest.

"I could show you a few of the trails and introduce you to the area, if you like?"

"I'd like that," she said, following his lead, trying to show up as well.

"Or maybe a swim if you're tired from traveling."

She shrugged, feeling a smile tug at the corners of her mouth. "Either one."

"Perfect. How about I come back around four?"

She glanced at her wrist and realized she wasn't wearing her watch. "That'd be great."

He nodded and put his hat on. His smile was so wide and gracious; it made her grin in return. "It's a date, then."

A surprising kick of adrenaline spread through her stomach. "It's a date," she finally said.

She watched after him until he disappeared into the

woods. The effect of him lingered, like a scent. Maybe it was because she had left the last of her grief on the dirt path that led her to this place. Or maybe it was something unique about him. She couldn't explain why. But she did know that her life would forever be changed for having met him.

GRIFFIN HIKED along the steep dirt path, his favorite trail that wound beneath the double waterfall. He could already hear its roar and the splash in the distance and he hoped the tourists weren't there yet. His day had started like any other day: responding to emails from students, preparing for the next archaeology class he would teach, and organizing his research for the dig in Greece he would hopefully work on. But he hadn't planned on meeting someone like Barbara. Beautiful, intense, and full of mystery.

He stared at the bits of blue sky that shone through the treetops, feeling like a firecracker had gone off inside of him —one that made him come alive and made him want to see her again. One minute she was street tough and world-wise, so fierce he thought she might pull a gun on him. The next minute she was soft innocence, so genuine and sensitive, she glided right past his emotional barriers. He checked his watch; he would make time to plan something special for tonight.

His phone rang and the caller I.D. said it was his cousin, lifelong partner-in-crime and, if luck was with them this time, successful business partner.

"Luke, hey buddy, what's up?"

"You need to start packing, that's what's up."

"Oh, yeah?" Griffin stopped.

"I heard from my contact in the permits department and it looks like we're getting approved this time."

"Get out. Are you certain?"

"Dead certain. They should be giving the college their notification later today. Which reminds me, I heard from Dr. Earhardt in the archaeology department. He said if this excavation goes the way we think it will, he wants us on the tour circuit—seven cities in Europe and twelve in the U.S. It could really happen for us this time, Griff. Uncovering this lost city is going to be a career-maker for both of us."

"Way to go, Luke!"

"Hey, I need for you to finish those new drawings of the lost city you were telling me about. Dr. Earhardt wants to try to use it as a sort of branding image on all of the media releases they send out."

"Alright, I'll send them this weekend."

"I need them tonight, actually."

Griffin looked down at the wide stream that flowed toward the falls. "Can't tonight. I've got plans."

"You're teaching a night class?"

"No, not teaching tonight. I'll do the drawing this weekend."

Luke sighed hard. "You met a girl, didn't you?"

Griffin thought about hedging on his answer and decided his cousin knew him too well. "I met a girl."

"Well, you're a member of the genetic jackpot club, you meet girls all the time."

"Not like this, I don't." Griffin started walking again. A gentle updraft curled around him with the damp, mossy scent of the forest. Footsteps sounded behind him and he stopped, turned, but didn't see anyone.

"How different could she be?"

"I don't know yet, I only met her briefly. All I know is

she's not like anyone I've ever met before and I'm going to see her again in a few hours."

"I doubt she's all that different from any other girl, Griff. Listen, you and I have had this thing planned since we were ten. Being archaeologists, making a major discovery, touring with the artifacts. We've literally talked about this for most of our lives. We've both given up a lot for this opportunity. This is it, it's finally happening. You need to get ready to fly to Greece."

Griff knew Luke was wrong about Barbara. There was a softness, a realness to her that most women he'd met didn't have. But he was right about how long they had chased this dream and how much they had given up. Luke had resigned from his prominent job in the archeology department at Emory when this project got its funding the first time. Griffin hadn't asked him to do that, but he hadn't complained when he did. It was Luke's tireless efforts that made this project come together. Griffin had given up this archaeological quest once, and that nearly killed him—and Luke. He'd let his cousin down before, he wasn't going to do that again.

"I'll be there, Luke. Nothing would keep me from it this time."

7

The man inhaled through his cigarette, then blew a curl of smoke from his position behind the cluster of evergreens. He raised the collar of his shirt around his neck, pleased with himself that he had found her.

He watched her gather her suitcase and a couple of over-stuffed tote bags, and load them onto the front porch of the small white house. She probably thought she was safe and hidden away. Yet she was alone, without protection and tagged with her husband's theft. David had been an idiot—stealing from the wrong people, then stupid enough to deny what he'd done. Barbara knew where those diamonds were, she probably had them with her. She must have left because he got too close. She would give them back, he would make sure of that. Then he would pass the diamonds to his boss, right after he took his cut.

It had been tricky to follow her up here without being seen. He'd rented a car, one she'd never seen before. He'd followed her around town, keeping his distance but watching her every move. Binoculars helped. But not as much as the GPS tracker he managed to slip into the back of the Jeep before she left town.

His phone buzzed from his back pocket. He walked down the dirt road so she wouldn't hear him.

"You find her?" the voice said on the other end of the line.

"Yeah, I found her," he said. "She's staying in Brevard, small house on one of the lakes up here."

"Chances are she has the diamonds with her. Just don't go into the house when she's there. Got it? Thanks to you the police are involved again. That's not what I wanted."

"You said you wanted me to find the diamonds no matter the cost."

"I said I wanted you to find the diamonds without getting caught!" His boss didn't yell, but the meanness in his tone told Elias he had lost his patience.

"You hired me to do a job. I'm gonna get it done. I don't need anybody telling me how to do things."

The man on the other end of the line shot one threat after another at Elias. He knew he was dead if he didn't finish this job. So, he had a new plan.

He'd gotten a real kick out of watching her sleep, standing over her in the dark while she was none the wiser. He shouldn't be scolded for how he handled things. He ought to be commended. He could have done anything he wanted to her on all those nights when he'd snuck into her home. She was right there, ripe for his picking.

She was such a pretty girl. All that soft brown hair and, though he'd never seen her work out, she looked fit. He had decided. This time he would finally take what he wanted from her. His sweet reward. Then she would be fully persuaded to cough up the diamonds.

"The fact that that husband of hers is dead is helping to

motivate her to hand over the diamonds," he said. "She knows we mean business."

"The fact that you killed him means that she's extra paranoid. Everything had quieted down, but now the cops are watching again. You made our job harder than it needed to be."

The two of them were quiet for a long time. Then Elias finally said, "I have a plan. I know how to get her to give up the diamonds."

His boss remained silent.

"Do whatever you have to do and don't get caught. This is your last chance," he finally said.

Elias hung up the call, got in his car and started the engine, he wasn't going to get caught. He checked the time. Very soon he would pay Barbara a special visit.

8

The sliding glass door at the back of the house framed Barbara's view of a lake that was nearly as blue as the sky. The unexpected beauty took her breath. This space, this little slice of heaven surrounded her with a sense of protection and feathery peace, like angels' wings.

She shut and locked the front door behind her, even though she didn't think she needed to be quite so careful here. She was well-hidden. Protected. She left her suitcase in the tiny foyer and walked straight to the back of the house. Kris had been right, the house was perfect.

There was one bedroom and one bath, which was all she needed. The living room was filled with a beige pit group that half focused on a big screen TV and half on the view of the lake.

She stepped cautiously onto the back deck and searched the area. Nothing but the scent of pine, beautiful evergreens and the peaceful sound of wildlife. Very different from the path that led her here. An egret flew overhead and splashed in the shallow water near the rocky bank. Owls hooted and birds sang and she thought with welcome relief that she had stepped into a world not entirely her own. One that belonged to the animals, to nature, and one that welcomed her as their guest.

Pop had been right when he told her that she needed to get out of the house. "Sometimes the memories don't do you any favors," he had said. "They tie up your heart and make you a prisoner of the past. It feels like your life is over. I know, I went through this when your mother died."

She texted her father to let him know that she had arrived. That she was safe. He responded by typing that the police were searching David's warehouse and their condo again in an effort to find the diamonds and any leads on the name Elias.

She filled her lungs with the mountain air, its cool fingers skimming the tension from her body.

She dialed Kris and told her about her next-door neighbor and the tour he offered her later in the day.

"He's that handsome?" Kris asked.

"Gorgeous," Barbara said. "But, I'm wondering. Maybe it's not fair for me to spend time with him. Not with all the chaos that's tethered to me right now. I mean, I wouldn't want to put Griffin in danger, too." She thought for the ten millionth time how David begged her to leave the country and she hadn't. She wondered if he would still be alive if she had agreed to travel. She shook her head to clear the thought.

"I think you're getting a little bit ahead of yourself. Don't you think? He's not asking you to marry him, you're just making a new friend. Go have fun. Enjoy the conversation. And the scenery." Kris giggled.

Barbara realized she was overthinking, still stressing. Kris was right. She needed to enjoy this little break. Let the police do their job. Maybe Elias would see how the police searched the warehouse and realize that no one knew where the diamonds were.

"Besides, you have to, so I can live vicariously through you. Now just enjoy yourself, I'm taking care of Pop while you're gone. Oh, and I got an email from Stephen. It doesn't look like the Army is going to let him come home early for the baby's birth."

"Oh, Kris. I'm so sorry."

Her sister-in-law sighed hard. "Me, too. So, go have a good time while you can. Before I'm too pregnant or over-whelmed with Mommy duty to give you another break. Send me an update tomorrow on how it went."

Barb said she would, hung up the call and decided to inspect the house. As safe as she felt here, she still needed to be smart. With her gun in hand, she checked the locks on every window and door. She also looked into the closets and searched the walls for small storage areas. She found none. She even searched the attic and, thankfully, didn't see anything suspicious.

She opened her suitcase and eyed the tumbled mess of clothes. That night came back to her—the creak of Elias' footsteps, her wrists taped behind her back, the massive hole between the two condos. The memory fueled a sense of rage. He had wrecked her life, and after she had fought so hard to overcome the cancer, to have a new beginning with her husband. No, she wasn't going to stay inside today. Kris was right yet again, she needed to step out and meet Griffin. Life was short.

She reached for a pair of shorts and reminded herself that she hadn't felt any negative vibes from her new neigh-bor. Then she remembered she had missed a few key points about David. And that came back to haunt her.

By the time four o'clock rolled around, Barbara had showered and changed into a white T-shirt and a pair of jeans. Her red bikini strings were tied in a bow at the back of her neck. She'd only been able to find one hiking boot, though, so she opted for tennis shoes.

She glanced out the back window now and then, searching for signs of the man in the ski mask who haunted her thoughts. She would know those eyes if ever she saw them again. When the knock came, she jumped, body and soul. Her hand gripped the gun that had been sitting beside her like a guard dog, the steel cool beneath her fingers. She parted the living room curtains to get a look at the front porch. Her new next-door neighbor faced the door in tailored shorts, and a fitted T-shirt. She exhaled slowly and returned the gun to her purse. No one was going to find her up here. She needed to relax.

"I'm an archaeology Professor at Brevard College. The campus is downtown, you might have passed it on your way out here." He gestured toward the road she'd probably driven earlier in the day.

She nodded. "Have you worked there long?" Her tone was cautious, careful, but confident. She had a practiced way with people.

"About five years, I guess. Good school. Great baseball team. Nice folks. Beautiful area. I'm an archeologist by trade. I teach for half the year, and my cousin Luke and I have a project we're pursuing in Greece."

"Beautiful home," she said as they walked by the side of his house.

"Thanks. It's an older home. I spent some time fixing it

up, knocked out a few walls to open up the inside, replaced the entire back of the house with windows." He pointed, still proud of his handiwork. "Being up here took some getting used to. You know, more animals than neighbors. There are only five of us up here, it's a lot different from living in town. But the quiet is good for my research, and you can't beat the scenery. The hiking trails and the waterfalls are epic, even healing on some level, I'd say. So, I can't complain."

She nodded slowly, like she was filing away every bit of information he shared, perhaps building a profile. He had the sense that once she thought she had him figured out that it would be hard to change her mind.

"What about you? What do you do with your time?" he asked.

"I'm an aesthetician," she said, lips pressed together in a tight smile.

"You're up here for a conference? Or—"

She shook her head. "Just a short vacation."

"You like to travel?"

"Love it. But I haven't done much of it in the last few years."

They stopped at the top of the hill and he pointed to his boat that was parked at the deepwater dock behind his house. "I thought a tour of the lake might be the best way to show you the area," he said.

He watched her look at the boat and then at the silver-gray lake that stretched into the distance, curving to the left at the foot of the mountains. Like a path waiting to be taken. "We could still hike if you'd rather do that. Or just swim."

"I think the boat tour is perfect," she finally said.

Griffin loaded the small cooler of bottled waters and snacks from the pier onto the boat and he watched Barbara come down the handmade wooden steps he'd built. Her long ponytail was pulled forward in a loose braid just below her collarbone. She was long and athletically lean, as if she had spent time running or playing sports.

It figured that as soon as he made plans to leave town, someone like Barbara would show up. From the first moment he laid eyes on her, he'd felt the connection. She was pretty, yes. Attractive in a way that grabbed a guy in the gut, made them look twice. But that wasn't the only thing he felt from her. He recognized something. As if they were the same, somehow. Like she was someone he could finally relate to.

He had taken the advice that Lillian had offered him some time ago—struck up a conversation, voluntarily offered up information about himself. Right from the start, even. Made himself more approachable, as she had suggested. "A woman could be intimidated by you, Griffin," Lillian had told him. "You have to help relax those barriers if you want to get to know someone again." But Barbara had told him nothing about her life in return. There was a story there, a twisted one, he suspected.

She had looked so scared when he first saw her, he'd thought she was about to pull a gun on him. Several times he had seen her touching her left ring finger with her thumb, as if she were accustomed to wearing a ring there. He'd done the same thing, too, and for a while, after he took his wedding ring off.

But that particular look of fear in her eyes. He had seen it in his mother's eyes when he was young, when she had had to leave his father. That fear of being found, of being hurt and of losing everything you cared about. It was a scent, almost, one he could recognize at a hundred yards. She was running from something. He would help her, if he could. If she would let him.

"Welcome aboard!" He helped her onto the boat, her hand was soft and delicate inside of his.

"Thank you." Her smile was warm but guarded, friendly but slightly distant. *Protecting herself.* Just as his mother had done.

He started the engine and backed the boat out of the slip. "Have you been boating much?"

"Almost every weekend. There's a lake not far from— there's a lake I used to go to back home."

"Where's home?"

"Uh, it's just a small town. I doubt you've ever heard of it."

He turned the steering wheel and set a slow path to the main part of the lake. He wanted her to open up to him, to trust him enough to share with him what happened. If only because he knew if she did that, that she would be closing the door on her past. Then, maybe, she would be willing to explore this connection they shared. One he hadn't felt with any woman in a long time.

"Are you Jewish?" He pointed to the Star of David keychain in her hand.

"Oh." She looked at it as if she had forgotten that it was still in her hand. "No." She paused as though she weighed whether or not to share anything. "My husband was," she finally said.

He nodded slowly, accelerated the boat into the open water. "He stopped practicing?"

She shrugged. "He died about a year and a half ago."

"Oh, I'm sorry."

"Thanks." She turned her face into the wind, toward the sun.

"My wife died two years ago," he said.

"I'm so sorry," she said, and he knew she meant it. She

would know how horrible that process was.

Now he knew at least part of what they had in common. They had both loved and lost. Her loneliness mirrored his own.

He pointed out the different neighborhoods that bordered the lake, where she could rent a wave runner, where she could shop and which mountains had the best hiking. When they reached the middle of the lake, he cut the motor, letting the boat rock and bob.

"How did she pass?" she asked the question easily, as someone did when they were intimately familiar with death.

"Lung cancer," he said. "She grew up in a house where her dad smoked. Vicious disease. She caught it at Stage 3, took the drugs, had the chemo, didn't make any difference in the end."

She winced. "My mother died of breast cancer. Got into the bone before she caught it and they couldn't save her."

Too many bad memories flooded his mind as usual. Some he could put in the time-will-heal box, others burned like salt in a fresh wound.

"How did your husband pass?" he asked.

She drew in a deep breath and shifted in her seat. "It was a— An accident."

He nodded, looked out at the smoke topped mountains that surrounded them on all sides. He opened the cooler and handed her a diet cola.

"Thanks," she said with a smile.

"Are we always going to be like this?"

"Like what?"

"I ask you a question to get to know you better, only you don't answer it and I end up not knowing any more about you than before." He tilted his head to the side, offered her his most friendly smile and wondered what had her locked up so tight.

She looked at the can of cola and ran her thumb around the rim. When she looked at him her blue eyes sparkled beneath long bangs. Her closed-lip smile told him she wouldn't be sharing any secrets today. He would have to work harder if he wanted answers.

He opened a plastic container of buckeyes that Lillian had dropped off earlier and offered her one. "Let me guess, you're running from the law? Wanted for murder?"

"Yeah, that's it." She laughed and took one of the buckeyes.

"It's alright. You don't have to tell me," he said.

She studied him for a moment. The water lapped at the sides of the boat. "I'm just getting some much needed R&R. Getting off the grid for a while."

He knew she wasn't telling him the truth and he had an overwhelming urge to help her, to protect her. To stand between her and whoever she was running from. He pulled a card from his wallet and wrote his cell number on it. "Here's my number if you need anything. I'm right next door if you need help."

Her shoulders dropped an inch. "Thanks. I appreciate that."

Griffin started the engine and circled the rest of the lake, showing her a few of the better restaurants, as well as an old stone church that had been built before the Civil War.

When the sun began to slip behind the mountains he asked, "May I take you out for dinner?" He thought for sure she would say no.

After a moment, she nodded. "That would be nice."

With one leap of his heart, his world spun to the positive. He knew exactly where he would take her.

9

B arbara studied her open suitcase that rested on the bed and tried to figure out what was different. She couldn't put her finger on what it was, but something was amiss.

She'd left her clothes in a tumbled mess, so she couldn't be completely certain. But something felt off. There were several pairs of her underwear on the bed. She didn't remember doing that. Her blue bikini top was laid out over the top of the suitcase. She didn't think she had done that either. Panic skipped through her heart at the thought that David's murderer might have found her.

She walked the rest of the small house, searching for signs that someone else might have been in the house since she had arrived.

The phone rang and she jumped. Pins and needles pricked her scalp.

Caller I.D. said it was her father. "Hello?"

"Barbara, you're there?"

"I am," she said.

"Honey, I've got Agent Hernandez on the line, do you have a minute?"

"Yeah, sure." She lowered herself onto the edge of the lumpy couch.

"Barbara, I was just letting your dad know that we have a match on one set of the fingerprints from the storage area in your condo. He's a long time criminal, been around Charlotte for a while. Did a short stint in the Miami prison system for breaking and entering, car theft, seems to have a talent for breaking into things. He was released from prison last year. No known employer."

"No surprises there," her dad said.

"His name is Elias Roberts."

"Elias," she said. "He owns the condo next to mine?" Barbara asked.

"No, the condo was purchased a little over a year and a half ago, by an LLC called Club East. They own several condos around Charlotte that they rent out," Agent Hernandez said. "We're looking for a connection between them and David's business, but right now it looks as though they just own rental properties."

"Did David ever mention anything to you about coming into some unexpected cash? Or did your lifestyle suddenly change?" Agent Hernandez asked.

"No. I'd been sick and we hadn't done much of anything for a long while. He did talk about travel. At the time I thought that was just about seeing the world, but then I found those passports he had made up for us."

"Your dad told me about those. Frank, I'll be by tomorrow to pick those up from you," Agent Hernandez said. "Barbara, we'd like to search your condo again."

"Help yourself. My sister-in-law is having some of my

things packed up. She can give you access. I'll email you her number."

"I can let you in," her dad said. "I'll meet you there and hand you the passports."

"Okay, let's meet there at nine tomorrow morning. Barbara, did you find anything unusual around the house? Paperwork for an account you don't recognize? Or can you remember David mentioning a hiding place?"

"No accounts. Just the safety deposit box I told my dad about which is where I found the passports. There was also a key in there that I didn't recognize. There weren't any numbers on it, and the banker said she didn't think it belonged to their bank. Is there a way to find out what it belongs to?"

Agent Hernandez was still trying to qualify whether David had stolen the diamonds. Barbara was already convinced that he had. She wondered if she found the diamonds and was able to give them to this Elias guy, if he would just leave her alone. Or if she gave the diamonds to the police, if Elias might kill her. He seemed like the type.

"I'd like to take a look at the key," Agent Hernandez said. "Without unique identifying characteristics, it might be hard to determine what it fits. Email me a photo of the key and let's give it a shot." Agent Hernandez said he had a warrant out for Elias' arrest, and he cautioned Barbara to be careful, to be aware of her surroundings. He said he would email her a photo of the guy and that he would contact the Brevard police and ask them to keep a lookout for him. "It's a small town, they would probably have time for some extra police presence in your area. The park rangers might be able to help keep an eye on you and your place as well. I'll ask and see."

After they hung up, Barbara stared at the lake. But she

didn't see the water. Instead she watched the memories of her life with David while they floated across her mind.

David had been her husband. Wives were supposed to know their husbands. She could read nearly everyone else she met with startling clarity, how could she have missed this about him? How had she not picked up on some clue that David had stolen diamonds? That he had even wanted to do such a thing? At the very least that he was up to something. And where would he have hidden them? She never believed that she was capable of hating David, but she was there today.

She focused on the man who broke into her home, whom she now had proof was Elias. Remembered the coldness in his eyes and the feel of his gun against her head. Subtle pieces of information reached for her, like a hand in the dark. David had said Elias was acquainted with one of his customers. He knew where she and David lived. Killed David because he'd stolen the diamonds and wouldn't give them back. Then searched the far corners of their house while she slept unaware.

Agent Hernandez asked if their lifestyle had changed. She'd said no and that was true. It hadn't. They had always lived conservatively. But David had paid off some pretty steep hospital bills without complaint. When she'd asked him about that he'd simply said that he'd taken care of them. She thought that meant that he had negotiated a discount. Perhaps not.

She knew Elias was obsessed with finding the diamonds. That he thought she had them. At least he'd lost track of her.

Or had he? She looked toward the open door of her bedroom, thought about her clothes that had seemed like they had been rearranged.

She could feel the heat of his stare from the other night, and her adrenaline continued to surge. She paced around the couch and inhaled deep, slow breaths. He wouldn't find her up here in these mountains. Certainly not in this preserve. She had been careful to make sure she wasn't followed.

She picked up the small key that David had left in his private safety deposit box and traced the ridges with her finger. She imagined stacks of money lined up in rows and black velvet bags full of diamonds packed into the metal box. Somehow she would figure out where that box was.

She peeked through the front curtains to prove to herself that no one was out there watching her. What she saw made her gasp.

Griffin walked across the front lawn, one hand in his front pocket, the other hand holding a bouquet of flowers. The goodness she had seen in him earlier in the day shone brightly in that moment. His facial expression in the unguarded moment, the way he sniffed the flowers, rearranged them a bit. The gentle smile that said he hoped she would like them. He had a Jimmy Stewart type of kindness, she decided, and it made her heart flutter and soften all at once.

WHEN THEY WALKED toward his house she expected to veer over to his dark gray SUV that was parked under a cluster of tall pines. Instead he guided her down the narrow dirt path they took to his boat earlier in the day.

"This way," he said, and pointed to a picnic table that was positioned on the bank of the cove. The table was covered with a white tablecloth, silver candle holders with ivory-colored candles had been placed in the center, and a picnic basket was perched on the end of one of the bench seats. "Welcome to Chez Griffin."

"You cook, too?" she asked.

He laughed. "Tonight it's lasagna. Hope that works."

"Couldn't be more perfect, actually. I love Italian food."

He set the plates and silverware on the table and poured the wine. She set her sights on the shadowy areas of the woods, looking for signs of movement. When she saw nothing, she turned her attention back to the lasagna. It smelled like it came from Mama Ricotta's, her favorite Italian restaurant in Charlotte.

The noodles were light and the sauce was both savory and sweet with just a hint of basil. Good grief the man could cook.

They ate and drank and talked until the stars above shone brightly. His gray eyes focused on her so intently she thought they might have taken her into their world. The wine, with its seamless blend of toasted spice and chocolate, left her feeling spellbound. Attraction hummed between them like a finely-tuned motor.

He asked her about the dreams she had for her life. This wasn't the normal small talk she expected and she put her fork down. He didn't realize it, but he asked her to talk about the secret wishes she kept hidden away. The ones she had kept close to her heart. The dreams she never discussed, at least not since her father had become so emotionally reliant on her.

But here in the semi-dark, with no one else to hear, and being certain that no one would find out what she said, she wanted to give them her voice. "I want to own my own business, a skincare spa. The best skincare at a reasonable price, so I can build a loyal clientele. I have it all laid out in my mind: light blue walls with soft music piped in to give clients an ethereal feeling, like a mini-vacation whenever they come in.

"Then when I've saved enough money, I want to travel. Everywhere. Particularly France, Greece, and Italy." She told him how she had put together a travel book of all her dream locations, how she had even mapped out sample tours and extended vacations.

"I think you'd be quite good at that," he said.

"How about you? What dreams do you have for your life?"

He told her how he and his cousin had dreamed of being archaeologists since they were kids, and how they had always wanted to make a truly fantastic discovery. Now, they were actually close to doing just that. "It's an ancient city that archaeologists have been in search of for the last few thousand years or so." His eyes lit up with an intense passion she'd seen only rarely. Sacred fire she called it. It was a special kind of excitement that came from childhood dreams. Her brother had it when he talked of enlisting. Her father used to tell her she had it when she talked about owning her own business.

"You found it?" she asked.

"We think so. I've been researching its existence for most of my career. Luke and I think it's in Greece."

He took her hand in his. Told her how long it took for them to narrow down the location of the lost city, how many misses they had over the years, how often they had to stop and regroup.

She looked at his fingers, felt the roughness that came from working in the elements. His entire approach toward pursuing his dream was methodical, precise. She'd seen that quality in law enforcement and lawyers, how they put clues together that led them to logical conclusions.

He described the dig site with such clear detail that she could see herself standing on the steep, dirt-covered hill that overlooked the bluest water she had ever seen. She could feel the warmth of the sun and smell the salt from the sea. Greece, she thought, a place she had always wanted to go. Then she realized what he was saying and her heart sank. He was leaving.

"You're moving to Greece?" she asked.

"It looks like it," he said. "Luke has finally gotten the business end of our excavation pretty well organized." His gray eyes held hers; their pull was magnetic and she couldn't look away. "There's something undeniable here—"

She looked at their hands together and she nodded. The chemistry between them was palpable.

He sighed and stared at the lake for a long moment. When he turned to face her again he said, "You've always wanted to travel to Greece, though, right?'

"My dad's health is not great, so I haven't traveled in a long time. He's had two heart attacks and I'm the only one around to take care of him."

"Ah." His hopeful expression fell. "Bad timing, then, I guess."

"Bad timing," she agreed.

They fell silent.

He looked at their entwined fingers, rubbed his thumb over the top of her hand.

"I'm glad to have met you," he said.

"Me, too," she said.

∾

THE WALK back with Griffin had been quiet. It was as if the two of them were supposed to catch an important train together but they had missed it.

Bad timing.

Once inside, she looked over the den. It wasn't her home so she wasn't completely certain, but, once again, she couldn't shake the feeling that someone else had been inside. She walked around, opening closet doors and checking locks. Nothing had been disturbed. No one was there except for her. The space just felt different, like someone else had been there. Paranoia, she decided.

"I'm the only one here now," she said aloud. But the thought of Elias being a master at picking locks left her feeling unnerved.

She poured herself a small glass of Bailey's and changed into yoga pants and a long-sleeve T-shirt. She snuggled into the corner of the pit group and covered herself with the white knit blanket that had been left on the back cushions, expected to fall asleep.

Owls and frogs serenaded her like they wanted her to let go of the past, let go of the stress, let go of the broken dreams. But she couldn't get Griffin off of her mind. He had burst into her life this morning like the sun, a bright light that mesmerized her, drew her close.

She found the pair of night vision binoculars her father had given her at the same time he had given her his Jeep, then went to her kitchen window where she had a clear view of the side of his house.

Griffin stood at the kitchen sink with a white tea towel over his right shoulder, scrubbing dishes. His red plaid sleeves were rolled up to his elbows and he rubbed his forehead with the back of his hand. His muscled forearms were spotted with clusters of soap bubbles. He hand-washed their plates and wine glasses, as well as the rectangular glass lasagna dish. She bit half of her lower lip.

There was a strength to him. A force. The authentic kind that came from navigating hardship. From surviving. Overcoming.

Barbara watched as he turned off the water and dried his hands on the tea towel. He sipped a glass of wine and stared toward the lake.

Goodness, she thought. That was the only way she knew to describe the quality she saw in him.

Goodness.

10

The knock came early.

Adrenaline skittered through Barbara's chest and down her arms. She popped up from the floor where she had been stretching into various yoga poses. She grabbed her gun from the coffee table, then peeked through the dining room curtains. An older woman with short and stylish white hair stood on the front doorstep with a bouquet of flowers.

She knocked a third time. "Yoo-hoo! Barbara? It's Lillian from the rental office. Your sister-in-law Kris sent me?"

Barbara slid the gun into the back waistband of her yoga pants, covered it with her shirt and opened the door.

"Hey, hon. I'm Lillian." She handed Barbara the flowers and offered a genuine smile. "Welcome to your home away from home. I usually stop by on the first day a new renter arrives, but I couldn't make it yesterday. The end of summer is bringing everyone into my spa to get their skin back in shape. Do you have everything you need, sweetheart? Plenty of fresh towels? Hot water heater working okay?" She craned her neck around Barbara and tried to see inside the house.

"Yes, ma'am. Everything's fine." The woman on her doorstep bore a slight resemblance to her mother—the gracious smile, the sparkling blue eyes, perfectly smooth skin. Her beaded turquoise necklace hugged the neckline of her floral print dress. Her entire appearance was put together to be deliberately soft and welcoming.

"Here's an extra key for you. You know, just in case." She pressed the key into Barbara's hand and patted it in a motherly sort of way. "And here's my business card. Call me anytime."

"Oh, thank—"

"Now Kris tells me that you work in a spa, facials and that sort of thing."

"Yes ma'am. Facials, lasers, waxing, no injections." Barbara suddenly realized how much she missed the morning routine of her work—getting out of the house, greeting clients, hearing about their lives. Routine could be a blessing.

"Oh, honey. Listen. I don't know if you're looking for some part-time work while you're here, but I could really use some help. If you're interested. I'll pay you half of what I charge for the service. You just let me know."

Barbara gave it a moment's thought. Lillian seemed awfully nice, and it would be good for her to have something to look forward to during the day. She got a bright, warm feeling in her gut speaking to Lillian. It was the kind of well-mothered sensation she felt whenever her own mother had hugged her, or listened to her problems or served her freshly baked cookies.

"Okay. Maybe I could stop by and see everything?"

"Of course. Now I don't have all the latest lasers like

what you're probably used to. My equipment is a little older —my clients like a good galvanic facial. But I think it's better than what they have out there these days. I have a very loyal client following, so I can keep you as busy as you'd like. Do you want to come by later today? I have clients all day, starting in about an hour." Lillian looked at her silver watch with a thin band. "But I could take a break around four and show you around then. Sound good?"

"That would be great."

"The salon address is on the card. I'll see you then." She walked down the front steps and waved. "Remember to call if you need anything. And, oh!" She walked back to the front door, placed her hand next to her mouth as if she had a secret to share. "Have you met Griffin from next door?"

"Yesterday, yes, ma'am."

"Oh, my." She fanned herself. "He works at the college, and he's an archeologist. He's our very own Indiana Jones." She winked and pointed to his house, like Barbara should make a move in that direction and fast.

Barbara stood on the front porch while Lillian pulled out of the driveway. When Lillian drove onto the main road she tooted her horn and they waved good-bye to one another.

Barbara paused, looked at Griffin's house. She wanted to see him again. But she thought about what he had said, how he going to move to Greece sometime soon. She shouldn't be disappointed. That would be jumping too far ahead with a man she had just met. She went back inside and put the spare key on the Star of David keychain. Her impression of him was strong and hopeful, kind and generous. She couldn't stop thinking about him, about the evening they shared. He was the first man she'd felt a connection with since David was killed. Though after what she'd learned about David recently, she wondered if she could trust her judgment of men.

She locked the front door, turned and caught sight of Griffin walking from his backyard down to the wooden pier. Once there he stretched tall, then tilted his head back, extended his arms wide and faced the lake. A pose of gratitude, she thought.

She stepped closer to the sliding glass door at the back of her house. He pulled his gray T-shirt over his head, and she caught herself staring at his physique. Her face flushed warm and she brought a hand to the side of her face.

Like someone tapped him on the shoulder, Griffin turned and faced her. She took a half step back even though she didn't think he could see her from his distance. But a smile widened on his face that told her differently. He gestured twice for her to come out and join him.

He faced her house with his hands resting on his hips, seemed to wait for a response from her. Sunlight played on the water that stretched ahead of him, like tiny golden angels dancing on the choppy water.

She looked at the key in her hand and ran her thumb over the Star of David keychain. She tossed it on the couch and stepped onto the deck.

"Mornin'!" he called and walked toward her.

She waved and leaned on the railing, she felt her happiness blossoming into a smile. He was leaving, she cautioned herself. And her life was too complicated at the moment. There was no way they could work out a relationship. But her heart ignored that fact. She was happy to see him.

He arrived just below the deck, he paused, his smile steady and honest. As if there was no hiding the fact that he was happy to see her, too.

"Thank you for dinner last night. You're quite the chef."

"You're very welcome." He bowed slightly, standing shirtless and tanned with a mystical quality to his gray eyes.

"It was perfect, actually. Reminded me of a favorite restaurant of mine back home."

His smile broadened another inch, and his gray eyes blazed, like his need for adventure were about to overflow. "What are you doing this morning?"

She shrugged. "No plans, yet."

"How about a hike and a swim?"

The idea of spending the morning outside with Griffin pulled her lips into a smile. He described the trail he was going to take, how part of it went by a double waterfall. When they made plans to meet out front, she realized she felt lighter than she had in a while. As if some sort of tether had just fallen away.

She remembered Elias, carefully weighed the safety of exploring her surroundings and being out in the open, exposed.

Griffin waved to her in an invitation. "Come on, we'll have fun."

She hadn't seen or heard from Elias. Maybe he finally realized she didn't have the diamonds, and had given up on her. Maybe he found the diamonds somewhere else.

"Okay," she finally answered. "I'd love to."

"Excellent." His smile widened. "We'll hike first, then swim. You'll love it."

"I'm sure I will," she said.

"I'll knock on your front door in about fifteen?"

"Sounds good."

Once inside she took a picture of the key she'd found in the safe deposit box and emailed it to her father and Agent Hernandez. Both men responded with the same message, "Got it."

She washed her face, decided against makeup since she would be swimming soon, then pulled her hair into a ponytail. She managed to find both pieces of her red bikini among the jumble of clothes in her suitcase. After she tied the top string to her bikini top she looked at herself in the long mirror and liked what she saw. She threw on shorts and a white, V-neck T-shirt and thought about how long it had been since she had done something like this with a man. Just a simple outing with someone who was interested in her. Years. She'd thought this part of her life had died with David.

Griffin knocked at the front door and Barb took the rental house key from the couch cushions.

"Ready?" he asked.

"I am."

She turned to lock the door, and caught sight of the gun she had left on the coffee table. She closed the door and locked it.

A moment later she reopened the door, grabbed the gun, shoved it into her purse and left again.

11

E lias watched while Barbara and her male friend made their way along the hiking trail. They were so focused on one another that neither thought to take much of a look around. Elias walked quietly and at a fair distance from them. Moved from behind one wide tree trunk to another to stay out of sight. The rich brown dirt on the forest floor was a cushion beneath his feet, made his steps soundless. His ankles brushed against the wide fern fronds that covered the forest floor.

When the path became narrow and steep, the man took the lead. Barbara followed close behind. When the trail widened again they walked side by side. They were a couple. For two miles Elias listened closely to their conversation, had hoped to hear Barbara mention something useful about the diamonds or their hiding place or plans to cash them in. She didn't.

He had searched David's warehouse, their home, their cars, the Jeep and now her luggage and the small house where Barbara was staying. No diamonds. The next step was one his boss wouldn't like. But it was what needed to be done.

With enough pressure, enough pain, enough motivation, people confessed. They gave you what you needed. He considered the remote possibility that Barbara might not know where David hid the diamonds. Unlikely but possible. Even if that were the case, she was still the best person to figure out where David had hidden them.

Elias slowed his pace, let Barbara and her new neighbor push on ahead. Then he doubled back. On his way to his car he thought about the contents of his trunk, compared them against his mental checklist. Duct tape to bind her ankles and wrists, ground-up oxycontin tablets to keep her subdued, a stun gun to use, if necessary. He took the gun from the back of his waistband and checked the barrel. Fully loaded. After a brief stop by his car, he would wait for her at her house.

WHEN THEY RETURNED from their hike, Barbara joined Griffin on his boat dock. He removed his T-shirt. Tanned and firm, she didn't remember any of her college professors looking like that.

"You know rumor has it that this lake was used as a baptismal for that church I showed you yesterday. One jump and the past is washed clean."

"Has it worked for you?" She slipped out of her T-shirt and shorts and adjusted her bikini top.

"Every day." His smile lit something in her heart that fluttered and kicked. It made her think of the fun, easy days of her teenage years, when she had her whole life ahead of her.

When she turned, he lifted his head with a jerk, as if he had been enjoying a long, slow look. She grinned at his guilty-as-charged expression.

He jumped in first, popping up a moment later and flipping his wet hair to the side.

She dove in next to him, the too-cool water hitting every nerve ending like a bucket of ice. "Oh!" she gasped.

His laugh echoed across the lake, bouncing off the mountains like this was their own private world.

"Thanks for the warning."

"It's invigorating!"

She cupped her hand and squirted a stream of water at his face.

They swam to the end of the channel and turned back before it opened into the wider body of water. Then Griffin flipped onto his back and gave her a perfect half-moon grin, one that was contagious and ignited her spirit of fun.

"Race?" she said and broke into a fast crawl.

She felt the current from his strokes close to her legs and she knew that she was only slightly ahead. Remembering her swim race days from her youth, she powered toward the pier at top speed, focusing on form and timing. When she slapped the top of the pier she lifted her head just in time to see Griffin a half-beat behind her.

"So close!" He was out of breath, his smile broadcasting enough electricity to fuel the town for a week.

She lifted herself onto the deck, enjoying the sensation that the work gave her muscles.

"You must have been a champion swimmer when you were younger," he said.

"My room at home is still full of medals and trophies. My dad can't bear to throw any of them out."

"At least I feel a little better about myself now." He laughed and lifted one of the seat cushions on the boat and threw her a towel. He took one for himself and slung it around his neck.

She dried her arms and legs and sat in the sun to dry out before heading inside.

He sat down beside her, leaned onto his hands, looking like a model from a Ralph Lauren ad. "The sunrise is tremendous. Comes up right over that mountain there."

"I saw it," she said. "I'm a morning person."

His smile was soft. "Me, too."

In the quiet moment between them, his magnetic stare returned. "There's something I've been wanting to do since we first met." He slid his hand to the back of her neck and settled his mouth on hers. Soft, slow, gentle.

With all the things that had gone wrong in her life, she was suddenly aware that he wasn't one of them. She inhaled the scent of his skin—a mixture of cedar and spice.

His tongue swept across hers. The grief and unbearable sadness, the chaos of stolen diamonds and gunpoint threats seemed miraculously far away. She wanted to live again. She pressed her hand to his bare chest, his curves solid beneath her touch. He sighed when her fingers trailed over the tight ripples of his abdomen, one, then the next.

He pulled back, ran his thumb over her cheek. "I don't know how to make this work now that I'm leaving."

His voice was low and its timbre hit a special chord inside of her, a part of herself that used to embrace the future.

"I don't either," she said.

They stood and he took her hand.

"Barbara—"

She turned to face him and a movement behind Griffin caught her eye. She looked at her rental house that stood on the hill behind Griffin. Panic hit her heart with a hard thump.

"What is it? What's the matter?" he asked.

"There's a man watching us. From inside my house."

12

S he grabbed the gun from her purse and ran up the wooden steps toward the house.

"Barb!" Griffin yelled behind her. "Barbara!"

She sprinted ahead. Even at a distance she recognized the man who had stood in the window. It was Elias.

Seeing him lit a fire of rage inside of her.

She was tired of suffering. Tired of crying. Tired of hiding.

She ran to the front of the house and found the door unlocked. With her gun drawn and aimed straight ahead, she stepped inside the house.

"Barbara!" Griffin grabbed her arm and pulled her onto the porch and out of the doorway. "Don't go in there! I've called 911, they're on their way."

"That man killed my husband, and he's threatened to kill me. He ruined my life once, I'm not going to let him do it again," she whispered.

"What? What are you talking about?" He grabbed her arm and bent low, tried to move her off of the front step.

Shots fired and Griffin spun backward, falling to the ground.

Barbara looked up in time to see the man moving out of the hallway and into her bedroom. She aimed and fired twice, hitting her target each time.

He fell with a hard thunk against the hardwoods, his black tennis shoes stayed toes down in the hallway. The rest of his body had fallen into her bedroom. She fired another shot into his leg, to make sure he wouldn't run. As she'd hoped, he didn't move. He didn't even cry out.

She turned and found Griffin standing, blood draining down his arm and over his hand. She ran to him. "Are you okay?"

Sirens screamed and a man yelled, "Drop the gun! Drop the gun!" She turned to find a park ranger near the bottom of the drive, pointing his gun at her.

"She's with me, Kurt! Don't shoot!" Griffin yelled.

She glanced at the man on the floor, the man she thought was Elias. One final check to make sure he wasn't moving. A pool of blood spread to the side of his leg.

She raised her hands, one of them holding her own gun. She hooked her finger into the trigger guard so that the gun hung loose, making it clear that she wasn't going to fire.

"I've killed an intruder." Her father had always told her that if she ever shot someone, that cops needed to know that she felt her life was in danger. They needed to know that right away.

"Griffin— What happened, son?" The park ranger kept his gun drawn.

"There's a guy inside." Griffin held his arm. "We were coming back from the lake and he started shooting as soon as he saw us.

Kurt stepped on to the porch and he took Barbara's gun.

"Let me see," she said to Griffin.

He removed his hand where the bullet had hit him.

"It looks like it just caught the edge of your arm. Dang it, I was afraid that something like this was going to happen." She helped him to the ground again, his face pale. "Here, sit down."

"I'm okay," he said, breathing hard. "I'm alright. What about the guy inside?"

"I killed him. It's over. He's not going to hurt you anymore." She wasn't sure if she was referring to Griffin, herself, or David. Maybe all three. The bastard wasn't going to hurt anyone anymore.

"He's dead alright," Kurt said from the doorway. "You hit him once in the chest, once in the abdomen. You a trained shot?"

She nodded. "My dad's a retired cop."

Kurt looked toward the sound of the sirens. Four police cars and an ambulance wound along the dirt road, lights flashing.

"I want to see him," she said.

"It's a bloody mess in there," Kurt warned.

The idea of seeing a dead man in the home where she had been staying made her chest tighten. But she wanted to see for herself that the man who had killed her husband, the one who threatened her, was indeed dead. "I can handle it."

He gestured for her to come into the house. His lips flattened as if this were against his better judgment. "Suit yourself."

She saw that her clothes had been tossed around the room, the lining in her suitcase had been cut. Elias had been looking for the diamonds.

He had fallen on his stomach, his head turned to the

side. She bent low and studied his face to get a good look. Aside from the picture that Agent Hernandez had sent, she had never seen his full face. Even if she hadn't seen the photo, she knew this man was him. The cold brown eyes were dead on.

"Do you know him?" Kurt asked.

Barbara shook her head. There was no sense in going into the long, sordid story. It was over. She headed toward the front lawn to see Griffin.

"Do you always carry a gun with you like that?" Kurt called after her.

"Usually," she said. "Carry permit is in the car if you need to see it."

Kurt shrugged like that wouldn't be necessary.

She turned and caught sight of several items on the bed —a stun gun, a light brown prescription bottle full of white powder and a roll of duct tape.

"Those aren't mine." She pointed to the items on her bed.

Kurt turned his attention to the bed, nodded. "Looks like he had a plan for you. We'll take everything into evidence."

She left the house, walked quickly toward the other end of the lawn where the EMTs sat with Griffin in the ambulance. One technician was taking his blood pressure, the other was inspecting his wound. She thanked her lucky stars he hadn't been killed.

Now that Elias was dead, that part of her past would drift into her history. The horrible ordeal was over. Without someone chasing her, she thought she and Griffin could spend some stress-free time together. Maybe she would be able to work out a short trip to Greece to visit him. Her dad would be okay with that timeframe.

Then she remembered Agent Hernandez telling her

about the LLC that owned the condo next to hers. The fact that Elias ended up living there made her realize that the owner of the condo and Elias were connected.

Fear snaked through her gut.

She glanced around the area wondering if that person was nearby. None of this was over. It wouldn't be over until the diamonds were found.

Griffin sat on a gurney inside the ambulance, a sympathetic smile lifting the corners of his mouth. "Our neighborhood isn't normally like this," he said apologetically.

She would have to explain how she was the reason that trouble had found him. He probably wouldn't want to see her after that. "Are you okay?" She took his hand.

He looked at the side of his arm. Rivulets of blood trailed along his skin. "Well. This isn't exactly how I'd planned our day."

"We're taking him to Regional Hospital if you want to follow us in your car, ma'am." The EMT stood as if he were ready to close the doors.

"Let's have a redo, tonight at my place. Sans guns and EMTs and so forth. Just wine and a fire and, apparently, take out." Griffin nodded to his arm where he had been shot.

She reluctantly let go of his hand.

"It's a date," she said.

13

"You're very lucky, Griffin," Dr. Johnson said and he threaded another stitch. "The bullet only took a chunk out of your arm. If he had been a better shot, this hole could have been in your neck. Or in a lung. Maybe even your head."

"I think the guy was a good shot," Barbara said from across the room. She remembered David being shot from a moving vehicle. Elias had been a marksman. "Griffin just moved at the right time."

The doctor looked at her over the top of his black-rimmed glasses, then returned his attention to Griffin's arm. "Well, that makes you doubly lucky, then. You might want to thank your lucky stars if this is the angel who's going to watch over you tonight."

Stars.

The doctor snipped the thread and dropped the scissors into a metal pan with a loud clank.

When the nurse began to discuss lab test results, prescriptions, and aftercare instructions with Griffin, Barbara went into the hallway. She called her dad and gave him the news: Elias was dead. Then he used his three-way calling feature and added Kris to the call, and she told the story all over again.

"See, this is why I taught my kids to shoot," her dad said with an air of validation. "In today's world you have to know how to protect yourself. I'll call Agent Hernandez and give him the news. Barb, are you coming home tonight or tomorrow?"

"Probably tomorrow," she said. "I'll have to figure out how to get all of my things out of that house. It's a crime scene right now."

"Where are you going to stay tonight?" Kris asked.

"I don't know. My neighbor got shot in the arm while trying to protect me and I think I'm going to help him for a little while. I'll figure it out." She ran her hand over her face, still unbelieving of everything that had happened. "Lillian, the property manager, probably knows of a good hotel or B&B nearby."

"I don't think you should be alone tonight," her dad said. He had reached the same conclusion that she had. Elias might not have been working alone and her whereabouts weren't the secret they had hoped for. "I'm going to have Agent Hernandez get you some police protection."

"I'll take it," she said. "Have him call me and tell me where to go."

She looked up just in time to see Lillian running down the hallway in her low-heeled shoes. She pressed her hand over her breasts to hold them in place. Her short hair was windblown and a look of worry painted her face.

"I'll text or call y'all later, I need to go," Barbara said.

Lillian gave her a warm hug. "Oh, honey, I heard all about it. I have a nephew on the force and he called me. Where are your clothes? Did you get blood on them?" Her questions ran together like one long sentence and her cinnamon perfume arrived two seconds after she did.

Barbara looked down at the doctor's lab coat and surgical shoe covers that one of the nurses had given her. "No, I had been swimming before I ran into the guy at my house. They wouldn't let me take anything from the house, so the nurses found me this hospital wear to cover up a bit."

"Oh, bless your heart. No, of course they wouldn't let you do that." Lillian dug through her royal blue purse until she found a pen and piece of paper, which turned out to be a grocery store receipt. She turned it over to the blank side and handed it to Barbara. "Write down all your sizes and I'll run by the department store and get you some things. You can stay with me tonight, and as long as you need. I have an extra bedroom and you're entitled to it. Mr. Grossman misses our children so much, he'll be thrilled to have more people in the house. I'll start working tonight to find you a new house."

She tried to refuse Lillian's shopping offer, but Lillian wouldn't hear of it. Barbara wrote down her sizes and told Lillian how she was going to see what help Griffin needed. Then she asked for a hotel recommendation. She wouldn't put another person in danger.

"Oh, honey, yes. Take care of Griffin." Lillian pressed her fingertips to her chest, her shiny red fingernail polish reflecting the overhead lights.

"You know Griffin well?" Barbara asked. She didn't want to pry, but Lillian gave the impression she knew everything about everybody. And even though Barbara didn't think she and Griffin had a shot at even exploring the connection they shared, she did wonder if her initial impression was correct.

"My husband works at the college so we've both known him since he moved here about ten years ago. Griffin is such good people. His wife died a while back. Right after she cheated on him. He's had it hard these last few years."

Barbara wanted to say thank you and politely make her way back to Griffin's hospital room. But Lillian took Barbara by the arm and sat on the bench on the side of the hallway as if she was about to share important, insider information. There wasn't a considerate way to exit the conversation just yet.

"Loralee, that was his wife, she cheated on him with Matt Robertson, who's the archaeology department head. He would wait until Griffin was on one of his archaeological digs and—"

The nurse wheeled Griffin into the hallway and whispered something to him that made him smile.

Lillian leaned close. "Oh, lookit. That's Blair; she's been chasing Griffin since the day after Loralee died."

Lillian trotted over to where Griffin sat and she gave him a gentle hug. She promised him a pot of her chicken bone broth soup, home-baked bread and an apple pie. She told Barbara that she knew these were all his favorites. Then she offered to go grocery shopping for him and said she would bring everything over before dinnertime.

Griffin nodded and worked in several polite you-don't-have-tos and a few thank-yous. He looked tired, but far too well to be in a wheelchair.

"Listen, sweetheart." Lillian held Barbara's hand. "I know we were supposed to have an interview today. But you just let me know when you want to work and I'll set up a time for you to come in. I know you'll be great. The clients will love you, I can tell these things ahead of time."

"Oh, well. Actually, I'm probably heading back home. Just as soon as I can recover all of my things from the house."

"No, that's—Oh, no. That just won't do. We don't normally have intruders like this." She squeezed Barbara's hand briefly and began to back away. "Griffin, talk her into staying. Just for a little while longer." She winked and waved like she patted something and headed out the door.

Griffin signed his discharge papers, collected his prescriptions, and the nurse helped him into Barbara's Jeep. "Remember to stay out of that lake until the stitches are healed," the nurse said with a call-me-anytime tone in her voice.

Barbara revved the engine slightly. When the nurse looked in her direction, Barbara gave her a half-smile.

She drove slowly along the winding mountain path, taking special notice of the steep drop to the right of the road. Dusk had settled over the mountains and she navigated the slippery gravel with intense concentration. She wasn't looking forward to driving back over this mountain in the dark to get to a hotel.

Elias was dead, but her gut screamed that this wasn't over. She checked her rearview mirror to see if anyone followed them. If whoever Elias worked with found her up here, and especially at night, it wouldn't take much to push her Jeep off the mountain.

Her throat went dry.

Elias' boss or partner would probably know by now that Elias was dead. Or at the very least that he hadn't found the diamonds. Someone else would come for her, to find the jewels David had stolen, she was sure of it.

Griffin leaned back against the headrest and they made small talk until they were almost to his home.

When they approached the gate, she slowed her speed. The light-haired park ranger seemed to recognize them, and came out of the gatehouse. Barbara rolled the window down. The ranger came close to the driver's side door and bent slightly at the waist to see Griffin.

His name tag read Calvin.

"You okay, Griff? Heard you had a little trouble today."

"Nothing we couldn't handle." Griffin waved.

Calvin looked at Barbara with slightly narrowed eyes, like he sized her up, like he wondered if she brought the trouble.

She recognized his expression, he considered her an outsider and a threat.

"Crazy world we live in these days," Griffin said, he put his hand on Barbara's knee.

Calvin noticed Griffin's hand. He stood upright, took a step back.

"Is this the only entrance into the park?" Barbara asked.

Calvin gave a sideways nod, and glanced toward the mountain behind him. "There are other ways in and out. They aren't advertised and they aren't obvious. But they aren't blocked off either. A conversation or two with the right local and you'd find your way to them. Of course if you're traveling on foot and not driving there are endless ways into the park. Why? Anyone we need to be on the lookout for?"

"I'm not sure," she said.

She didn't know how many people Elias worked with, how many people might be next in line to come after the diamonds, how many people might be tracking her. She had no idea who to be on the lookout for.

Calvin stuffed his hands into his pockets. "You let us know if you think of anyone."

"Thank you, Cal," Griffin said.

Calvin pressed a button inside the guardhouse and the gate raised slowly.

She drove toward Griffin's house. They passed the place where she had run into the bear and she noticed that her hands were tight on the wheel. She would have to drop Griffin at his house and leave quickly. As much as she wanted more time with him, she couldn't put him in any more danger and she couldn't get turned around on these roads at night.

"So, now might be a good time for you to tell me how you came to carry a gun in your purse, and why that guy was in your house. Don't you think?"

She bit her upper lip for a moment and glanced at him. His eyes were fixed on her and it looked like he wasn't going to settle for anything less than the truth.

She accelerated when the road straightened and decided that—no matter what—honesty was best. If David had done the same with her, he might be alive today.

"You're right. I'm sorry. I thought we could spend a little time together without my situation becoming a problem for you, too. Obviously I was wrong." She exhaled hard, faced the dirt road ahead and summoned her courage. "My husband was murdered. It wasn't an accident like I originally said. I thought I was hidden well enough way up here that no one would find me." She cleared her throat. "He was killed about a year and a half ago, while we sat outside at a restaurant. The guy who did it was never caught, but he broke into my home recently and put a gun to my head. He said that David had stolen some diamonds from him. He wants them back and he thinks I can get them for him."

She told him how David had an import/export business, and she thought he must have stolen the diamonds from one of his clients. She went on to tell him how Elias Roberts had rented the condo next to hers, and how he broke in through the firewall to search her home for the diamonds she had never seen. She told Griffin how Elias would kill her if he didn't get the diamonds back.

"I came up here to get out of sight for a while. My hope was that the police would have found him in short order. But he found me, instead. I'm so sorry. If I'd had any idea that he knew where I was, I wouldn't have accepted your invitation for hiking or dinner or anything. This isn't even my Jeep, I thought I'd gotten out of town clean."

He was quiet.

She pulled the Jeep into Griffin's driveway and parked next to his SUV. She shifted in her seat to face him, expected him to ask her to leave.

"You don't need to apologize." His tone was soft, understanding, and it took her by surprise.

"I want you to know that we think the guy I shot today might have been working for someone. That means someone else might know that I'm here, and he could come after me. I'm going to find a hotel for the night. There's a Charlotte FBI agent working on the case and he's going to have someone from the Brevard police force keep an eye on me tonight. I don't want to subject you to any more trouble. You've been through enough today." She nodded toward his arm.

He scanned her face like he was solving a puzzle, figuring her out. In the quiet she became acutely aware of the force of their connection. Every detail came alive in the small space of the car, the spiced scent of his sweat, the pulse of each beat of her heart, the fierceness of their attraction. Its intensity nearly took her breath away.

He placed his hand on hers, squeezed gently. "I think you're the one who's been through enough."

Her lips opened, a sigh escaped. The tension in her chest gave way to her heart which seemed to expand.

He closed the distance between them, slowly, until his lips nearly touched hers. "I don't think you should be alone tonight. Stay here. Let me watch over you."

She hesitated. "I don't—"

He pressed his lips to hers, stopping her objection.

"I want to," he finally said. "If you'll let me. I have several friends on the force, I'll get them up here to keep an eye on us."

She opened her mouth and his lips met hers again.

After a moment, he said, "And I'm sure, so don't ask me if I am. You'll be safer up here with me, than you would be alone in a hotel in town."

She felt her lips widen into a smile. "Okay."

His eyes combed the area, and she looked out to see the forest was dark with shadows that seemed alive. "We should go in," he said.

They walked toward his double front door and the cool pine-scented breeze sent yellowed leaves twirling across their path.

Griffin pulled his keys from his pocket and fit the house key into the lock. She caught sight of her rental house. Yellow tape had been wrapped around the small front porch. She slid her hand along Griffin's back, reminded herself that she had been right to trust Griffin, that Lillian had given her good validation on her insights.

Inside, Griffin's home was the perfect mountain house, a sophisticated log cabin with paneled walls and rosewood beams across the ceiling. The back of the house was mostly glass to bring the majestic outside in. His furnishings consisted of black leather couches with silver steel frames, and wall-to-wall bookshelves that were crammed full.

"Can I get you some tea?" he asked.

"I think I'm the one who ought to be catering to you, don't you think?"

"I'm fine." He shook his head, rolled his shoulder a couple of times. "They gave me a local injection so I actually don't feel anything in that spot right now. I might take some ibuprofen later. You don't have to fuss over me."

"Well, I should fuss a little. You wouldn't have a hole in your arm if it weren't for me."

"I don't have a hole in my arm anymore, they stitched it up. All I'm going to have to show for what happened today is a small scar, and an adventurous story to share with my students. I'll get to tell them I got shot and they'll think I really am Indiana Jones." He smiled his glorious smile and a little bit of her melted.

He guided her to take a seat on the longest couch. "You've been through a hard time. I know what that's like. I'm just glad that no one got seriously hurt today."

"Me, too." She exhaled deeply.

"Now. Doors and windows are locked. All entry points are wired to the alarm system. If the alarm does get tripped, the signal goes right to the police station. I have a gun in the bedroom that I'll bring out, so it's on hand." He stood and closed the blinds over the windows. She felt increasingly better as each set of blinds shut the world out.

"I know you have your gun," he said.

She patted the side of her purse. "I do."

"I'll call my buddy Mac at the police station right now so they can get someone up here before the gates are locked for the night." He paused and looked up like he examined a private, internal checklist. "I know this is a frightening situation, but I feel better about you being here than in some hotel by yourself."

"Me, too," she said.

She must have appeared somewhat overwhelmed because he sat next to her, quietly folding his hands.

"Diamonds, huh?"

She shook her head, still not used to the idea. "Apparently. I never picked up on what David had done. There weren't any buying sprees or new cars. No fur coats. He did pay off some steep medical bills that the insurance didn't cover. I just thought his business was doing well and that's where he got the money. I didn't know about any diamonds until Elias, the guy I killed today, showed up in my house and put a gun to my head."

He didn't flinch, didn't seem to judge or be surprised.

"You think you know someone, you think you can trust them. Then you find out you don't know them at all," she said.

"We all want to trust those we care about. Trust gives hope, it gives our life meaning, it gives us a solid foundation. When we realize our trust was misplaced, it's devastating." A painful memory flitted across Griffin's face.

Barbara remembered Lillian's story about Griffin's wife.

"My former wife had an affair. Betrayals are hard. Takes a while to trust again." His tone was cautious, like he wasn't quite there himself.

Barbara thought her ability to trust would come back just as soon as she could figure out why she had missed the fact that David was a thief. Not to mention a liar.

"Maybe one day we'll both get there," she said softly.

His gray eyes softened, and for a moment they gazed at one another. It was like they belonged to a secret club. They knew what it was like to love and to have lost, to have your trust betrayed, and to need to begin again.

"Now," she said after a moment. "The doctor said I

needed to watch over you tonight, but did he tell you what I was supposed to do?"

Griffin chuckled quietly like she had missed the inside joke. "That was his attempt to fix us up. He's been married to his wife Marianne for thirty-five years and he thinks everyone should be on that same path."

She gave a long nod and a short laugh. "Ah, Okay."

He walked to the kitchen and pulled a pitcher of tea from the fridge, along with a bowl of red cherries.

"I think everyone in town is trying to fix you up," she said, remembering Lillian's encouragement.

"They're good people, they mean well." He took two slim glasses from the cabinet, filled them with crushed ice, and poured the tea. "Lillian will be along soon with more food than we could eat in a week. But maybe these snacks will get us through until then. I think I could also scare up some crackers if I worked at it."

He handed her a navy blue Brevard College sweatshirt from the back of one of the breakfast chairs. "I'm sure you're tired of wearing that doctor's coat."

She took the sweatshirt from him and their hands slid against one another. "Thank you." She slipped the sweatshirt on. It was oversized, warm and soft, and it smelled like Griffin: seductive, like the forest that surrounded them.

"I think Lillian is bringing a few things for me to wear as well."

He raised an eyebrow at her lower half that was still clad in her bikini bottoms. "I think I like you in my sweatshirt better."

A grin pulled at her lips. "You're a terrible flirt."

"Not usually." His smile widened and he tossed a cherry into his mouth. "But I can't seem to keep my thoughts off of you."

He called his friend Mac, who agreed to provide police support for the night.

Happiness fluttered in her chest like the newness of spring. She ran her hand alongside a large and detailed model of what looked like an ancient city.

"So, this is it?" she asked.

He handed her a glass of iced tea and offered her a cherry from the bowl.

"Yep, my first big discovery. Hopefully, anyway. My theory is that it was covered by a volcanic eruption that happened about halfway through the second millennium. If I'm right, we ought to find this in Crete. Right now we're waiting for the final approval from the government in Greece to allow us to dig and explore."

"Lots to that process, I guess?"

"Quite a bit, yes. The government wants to make sure we don't remove anything that we find, they want all the artifacts to go to their museums. The college is trying to fund our trip, so we have to make sure they have the proper amount of money for the dig and so forth."

"So, one day I'll walk into a museum and I'll see a big, black and white photo of you in front of your discovery? You'll be wearing your Indiana Jones hat, of course."

He laughed. "Something like that."

She turned and found him closer than she anticipated. Attraction ignited between them like fireworks on Independence Day. She stepped to the side of the archeological display. "Do you have an Indiana Jones hat?" she asked softly.

He pointed to the rack in the foyer where several wide-brimmed hats hung in a row. Some were off white, some tan. "No fedoras. But those do the job."

Silence hung between them, and his gaze swept over her

face. She thought for a moment that he was going to kiss her again. But he cleared his throat and stepped away.

He talked about his ancient city, the years of effort he had put into trying to locate it, how much he loved Greece and Italy. His enthusiasm ignited her own. Reminded her of the stacks of travel books she used to check out from the library and the hours she had spent poring through them, planning the faraway trips she'd thought she would have taken by now.

She longed for that life of adventure she hadn't lived, the path she hadn't taken. New cities, new countries, new ideas.

The coolness of the moon's light shone into the room through a triangular window near the ceiling. The quiet, healing energy of the lake reached her. He took her iced tea glass and set it on the counter, then drew her into his arms. He pulled her into a kiss, opened his mouth over hers.

It was the first time in too long where she felt she could let go. The first time in quite a while where she actually wanted to feel the emotions that coursed through her.

His tongue swept across hers and his hands slid under the sweatshirt, running along her back. He pulled away. His gray eyes were fierce and dazzling.

He brushed his hand over her hair. "You've been a complete surprise to me." He smiled briefly and pressed his lips to hers in a kiss that was slow and long and deep.

She leaned into him. She had forgotten what this was like, to be so attracted to someone. That it could feel so right, that the moment could carry her away.

A warning sounded from the back of her mind—he was off to Greece for his expedition soon and she would have to go home to take care of her father. She stepped away.

He paused, appeared to study her face. "Do you want to take some wine into the sunroom?"

She bit her lower lip. She'd never felt so drawn to someone before, so captivated. All the months of suffering and crying. The endless nights of feeling lost and alone. That all seemed to burn away in the moment with him.

"I have a new French red we can try." The caress of his fingers was slow against her arm.

She drank in the heat and the fire that came with being so close to him and said, "I'd love that."

14

They sat in the sunroom that faced the lake; the curtains were drawn for privacy and safety. Frogs, crickets and the occasional coyote serenaded them from the outside.

"Tell me something about you." Griffin drank a sip of wine, gestured with his glass. His light gray eyes were clear and intense, studying her closely.

"What would you like to know?"

"Anything. I'm an archaeologist. I like discoveries. Tell me what you like, besides boating and swimming."

She traced the angle of his jaw with the tip of her finger, enjoying the prickle of his light beard. "I like the beach in autumn, the mountains in the summer, and pretty much anywhere in the spring. I love being near water and I'm always happiest when I'm outside."

He kissed her lips, then her neck. She wondered how long they could stay like this, adrift in their own world.

"Now you. Tell me what you like," she said.

He leaned back, exhaled deeply. "I'm happiest outdoors

as well, especially when I'm on a dig. I love to travel, I love waterfalls, and swimming in the ocean under a full moon."

"Mmmm, swimming under a full moon. I wish I'd thought of that one."

"Now, a tough question." He narrowed his eyes at her with pretend seriousness. "Tell me your secret psychic superpower."

She laughed. "What?"

"Everybody has one." He drank the last of his wine, put his glass on the coffee table. "For example, mine is finding things. I can find almost anything. Lost, buried, stolen, if I have enough clues to work with, I can usually find what I need."

She thought of the key and the Star of David keychain her former husband had left behind, and wondered if Griffin could help her find what the key opened.

"Then being an archaeologist is a good fit for you."

"It is a well-suited career. Okay, your turn."

She thought of her uncanny instincts. She didn't typically tell people about them, but she wanted to open up to him. "Well, this may sound rather strange, but I can tell a lot about a person as soon as I meet them."

His eyebrows climbed and he shifted his weight to the side. "Okay. Like how? Show me how that works."

"It's not really something I can show, it's more of a gut feeling."

He leaned forward slightly, obviously interested.

She explained it as best she could. "I don't get details or personal histories or anything like that. But most of the time I can get pretty useful information about what someone is like. My dad likes to joke that no one is a stranger after a minute with me. It's all just about paying attention to energy and little tells, I think. Watching for those subtleties that everyone gives off. I read them well."

She thought of David's fake passport and driver's license. "Typically, anyway. My former husband was the exception. Strangely, I never could get a handle on him. Pop always said I'm too much like my mother, I like to see the best in people, so I overlook things when it comes to people I care about. Important things like flaws, tendencies, motivations. People surprise the heck out of me if I don't pay attention to my instincts. David was the only person I'd ever met that I couldn't read at all, but I loved him, so I gave him the benefit of the doubt."

"Any idea why that was the case?"

"None," she said. "Just before he was shot, he told me he thought he knew why I couldn't read him, and he was going to share that with me. But he never got the chance."

"Another mystery," he said.

"My dad used to introduce me to people when he worked police investigations years ago."

"You helped him solve cases?"

"A few. I could tell if someone was lying or acting guilty. It wasn't admissible evidence, obviously. But sometimes my input was useful for him, it helped to point him in the right direction."

"Fascinating."

She nodded, smiled.

After a moment he looked away and the quiet stretched between them. Without Griffin's upcoming move to Greece, exploring what was next would have been easier. As it was, his move was the elephant in the room. It stilted their progress. She thought she sensed a resoluteness from Griffin. Not just about his move, but maybe about his relationship with his cousin as well. It was something in the way he discussed Luke. She decided that since there was no way around the topic, she would choose a more direct approach.

"Tell me more about your cousin and this project y'all are working on." She sipped the last of her wine. Griffin refilled both of their glasses, clicked his tongue against the roof of his mouth.

"Well, we've been planning this discovery for decades. Literally. Luke got two masters and a Ph.D. all relating to archaeology. It's like our whole lives, our entire relationship has been leading up to this moment. Luke is terrified that I'm going to back out of this project, in part because it's taking him so long to get everything organized."

"And the other reason?" she asked.

"I stood him up twice before," he said. "The first time I was supposed to go, my former wife and I were having some difficulty. I'd been traveling a lot. She asked me to give up the digs and the project with Luke. I did, to try and work things out with her." He shook his head. "But giving all that up didn't help the marriage. So Luke and I rebuilt the project. Then she got sick the next time I was supposed to go. I stayed here to take care of her. By the time she passed and I thought I could work again, our permits had expired, and we were back to square one."

Barbara thought of what Lillian had told her about how Loralee had cheated on Griffin when he traveled for work. When she got sick he took care of her until the very end. *Goodness.*

"Were you and your wife happy? Before she got sick?"

He looked beyond her like he took the question seriously and needed to find just the right answer. "For a while. But I wasn't happy without my work. Thought I could do without it, but I couldn't. I needed my archaeological work like I needed air. That meant traveling and being away from home for months at a time. We talked about it at length. She tried traveling with me and hated it. So, we tried it apart— she stayed home while I traveled. But my being away was hard on her. Ultimately I don't think long-distance relationships work."

"She tried to be what she thought you wanted and lost herself," Barbara suggested.

"That's about right," he said. "Loralee was a very pretty girl, and she relied on those looks too much, not enough on what she had inside." He tapped his chest. "As a result, I don't think she ever really figured out what she wanted. She liked the attention she got from men, she tended to follow that favor whenever it was presented. In a small town, a pretty girl has lots of options."

"I'm sorry. Life is so hard sometimes."

"Yeah. Well. I guess we've both learned that. Lillian tells me I've isolated myself, that I need to be more outgoing, more involved at the college and all of its social activities."

Barbara smiled at Lillian's suggestion. She had been told the same thing by family and friends. she never followed their advice. "What do you think?"

"Eh, she's probably right. I ought to get out more, but being an archeologist, traveling, it's all I've ever wanted to do. My idea of getting out will be going to Greece and working on the dig." His voice faded and he rubbed his thumb along the edge of her bottom lip.

A breeze hummed through the trees. A subtle scent of pine and camellias drifted into the room. She thought of the wish book she had put together, with all of the pictures of faraway locations she had collected over the years. Her travel bucket list. Greece was on the front cover, but now that location seemed further away than it ever had before.

"So, um. Did your gut tell you anything about me?" he asked.

"It did." She nodded.

"And what did it say?"

She ran her fingernail down the center of his chest. "You're a good person, Griffin."

His expression softened.

She placed her hand over his heart. "You honor your commitments, you play by the golden rule, even when it doesn't benefit you. You love your work so much that you would work day and night if you could get away with it, you think that if you hadn't been traveling that you and your wife might have been happy."

Griffin rubbed his hand across his forehead. "Wow. That was...crazy accurate." He stared at her, his mouth slightly open. He turned toward the window for a long moment, as if too many thoughts tumbled through his mind.

There was a rustling that came from what sounded like the driveway. Then the noise of a car engine starting.

When Griffin finally turned around, he said, "Come on. I think Lillian left some things for us on the front porch."

He looked out the door viewer, then unlocked and opened the front door. They saw Lilian's rear taillights as she pulled onto the main road. On the front porch they found three bags with the items Lillian had promised: hot soup, homemade bread, pie and several outfits with the tags still attached.

Barbara selected a pair of dark jeans and a denim button-down that Lilian left for her.

After she changed her clothes she met Griffin in the kitchen, "Is it really true that you can find anything?"

"Just about anything." He selected a new bottle of wine from the wine rack. "Are you trying to find something?" He lowered the bottle to the counter slowly, as if he suddenly understood the nature of her question.

"David left behind a key. It might be a safe deposit box key, I'm not sure. It doesn't belong to the bank we used." She served two bowls of Lillian's soup along with the warm bread. "I'm wondering if that key fits the place where he left the diamonds."

His gray eyes lit up. He was ready to help, ready for a challenge, ready to uncover what had been hidden. "Tell me what you have so far."

They sat at the breakfast table and she glanced at the uncovered window near the ceiling, bright stars covered the evening sky. While they ate she told him about the fake passports she'd found and how David had pushed for them to leave town.

"May I see the key?" he asked

She dug into her purse and pulled the Star of David keychain from the zippered pocket. "Here it is."

He turned the keychain over in his hand, examined both sides. "After death, everything people have left behind is a clue. Sometimes it's intentional, other times not. So, let's think about this. Did he leave a note with the key?"

She shook her head. "The key was in a safe deposit box that I didn't even know about. The banker alerted me to it. Although David was a very deliberate person." She told him how he had given her instructions about the safety deposit key and box. "I think he had to know that if something happened to him, that I would find the other box, and this key."

"Okay, then, let's figure out what he was trying to tell you." He held the Star of David keychain. "Could be a simple reference to his name, or his faith—"

"He was more intentional than that. If David left this

symbol behind, I think he intended for me to discover some meaning behind it," she said.

"Right. Of course. The symbol certainly has lots of meanings on its own. Hang on just a second, I need some paper." Griffin walked into the kitchen where he opened and closed cabinets, rummaged through drawers.

His text alarm sounded and she glanced at the message that illuminated his phone screen.

It was from Luke: I have verbal confirmation that permits have been signed. Should have them in my hand by Friday. You need to get your ass over here pronto. Workers can be ready to start by Monday!!!

Hope that she didn't even realize she had fell from her heart and sank into an all-too-familiar pit of disappointment. She reminded herself that she had only known him for a few days, that she shouldn't feel disappointed. But she did.

Griffin had reminded her of her dreams, the life she'd once thought possible and who she was deep inside. That part of her wasn't dead and gone as she had often thought. It was still alive and wanting a place in the world.

Griffin returned with a notepad and pencil and he began to write. "This particular type of star was the central symbol for the Zionist community, then the Jewish community after the 1890s."

"It's a hexagram," she said, remembering some of what David had discussed with her about the different types of stars. "Often used in the occult."

Griffin wrote down what they each said.

"The star is made up of two triangles," she said and traced the upright triangle with her finger. "The first is considered a phallic symbol, an icon for male. It stands for aggression and manhood. The second triangle is considered the female symbol, it's the exact opposite. Could be considered the cup, a vessel, a woman's womb."

The text alarm dinged for the second time and Luke's message illuminated on the screen again. Griffin read the text, he cleared the preview from his screen.

"Or the more traditional symbolism of the hexagram is God reaching down to man, and man reaching up to God. Or you can see it as just a star, which has an association with the heavens," she said. "In some spiritual communities stars are seen as symbols of the battle between light, which refers to the human spirit, and darkness which relates to material forces. After World War II it became both a symbol of martyrdom and heroism."

Griffin looked at her, his eyebrows raised. "You do know a lot about stars."

She told Griffin about David's obsession with stars and how they covered the interior of their home. "We discussed their meanings ad nauseam. He loved their imagery. When he learned that I had studied the constellations with my mother over the years, he took this common interest to a whole new level, putting stars all over our home. He called them 'little bits of light God dropped from the heavens to guide us on our way.'"

"To guide," Griffin pointed out. "So, the stars have always been clues somehow. He planted clues for you. Just in case."

"Now that I have this key, and a lot of hindsight, I think you're right. The stars have to be clues for me to find the diamonds. He asked me about Elias on the day he was killed and gave me some story about him hitting on men's wives. I think he made that up, but suspected Elias of something worse."

Griffin stared at the small key. "Safe deposit box key. Probably, anyway. Star of David." He traced the two triangles with his middle finger. "What banks do you have in your area?"

"I'm from Charlotte. We have more banks than churches, and we have an awful lot of churches. None that fly the Star of David as their logo, though."

"I've actually spent a lot of time in Charlotte, and I don't remember any banks with stars, either. Alright. Let's figure this out. Light, dark, God, man, heaven, hell, martyrdom, heroism—"

"Opposites," Barbara interrupted. "That's it. This star, its imagery is all about opposites."

Griffin nodded. Wrote the word opposites on the notepaper and circled it.

Barbara grabbed her phone and googled banks in Charlotte. She studied the long list of results.

"We talked endlessly about the different types of stars, their meanings, where they show up in history, in architecture." She pulled up one website after another and examined the buildings.

Griffin took the lower half the list and did the same.

After almost an hour of searching the images Griffin said, "Maybe they got to him before he could give you a more obvious clue."

"I think he didn't put the more obvious clues out because he was afraid someone would break in and find them."

"You're probably right." Griffin picked up his phone and resumed his search. "Let's stay at it. Something will jump out."

They each scrolled through page after page, their eyes focused and searching the images and architecture of every bank in Charlotte.

Barbara sat up straight and pointed at the screen. "This one."

Griffin leaned over. "Regional Bank of Charlotte? Why that one?"

He typed in their website address and enlarged the front page on his phone. "I know this bank. It's close to UNC Charlotte, where I taught a few classes once, and I remember this building."

"Look at the fountain out front," she said. "See how it has a flame in the middle and the water sprays around it?"

"Opposites," he said.

"Right. And you could say that the fire and the water are representative of—"

"Male and female energies," he said quickly.

"Exactly," she said. Chills covered her arms. "That's it. I'll go there in the morning."

"I can go with you, if you like," he offered.

"Really?" Hope expanded in her chest and she tried to temper it. Having him along would be incredibly helpful, since he had an expertise she didn't have. And she wanted more time with him. But he was supposed to be on his way to Greece. Never again would she hold someone back from leaving town.

"You have time?"

He put his phone in his pocket and nodded. "I'll make time."

"Okay," she finally said. "I'd actually really appreciate that." Her phone rang and caller I.D. said it was her father. "I need to take this."

"I'll give you some privacy." Griffin stood and waved his phone. "I have to text Luke, anyway."

She answered her phone as Griffin walked into the next room. "Hi, Pop. You okay?"

"I'm fine, sweetheart. Are you someplace safe?"

"Yeah, I'm at my neighbor's house."

"Okay, hang on just a second." There was a beep, then her father said, "Agent Hernandez, are you there?"

"I'm here, Frank."

"Good. Did that right. Barb, I did some research on this Club East that owns the condo next to yours, and they were on David's customer list up until about a year ago."

Barbara's heart beat against the inside of her chest with both fists.

Pop had kept David's business going since David died. They had discussed the idea of selling it, but it really wasn't big enough for that. There was enough steady business and long term clients that it pretty much ran itself. It gave Barbara a steady income. And there wasn't much to do to keep it running other than open the doors each morning, send out a few invoices and paychecks each Friday. File a tax return at the end of the year. It was enough work to make Pop feel useful and not so much that it would tire him out.

"We discovered that another LLC owns Club East," Agent Hernandez said. "Ajay Ravi is listed as the primary owner."

"David must have taken diamonds from one of their shipments and got caught. They probably came after him when he didn't give them back," her father said.

Barbara looked at the Star of David keychain that Griffin left on the glass table and she put her fingers over her mouth.

"This means that our suspicions were true. Elias wasn't operating alone," her father said. "And that means that this Ajay Ravi, if he's the one that Elias was working for, probably knows where you are. Maybe not specifically, since you're not in that same house anymore. But I would suspect that he knows your general location."

She grabbed the shirt at her chest, feeling paranoid. "Do you know what he looks like?"

"I'll email you a copy of his driver's license," Agent Hernandez said.

"You should come home," her father said.

"If he knows where I am and he follows me, that will lead him right to you. I can't do that."

"I'll have several cops to keep an eye on us. There's no safer place you could be than home," her father said.

"I sent the Brevard P.D. Ajay Ravi's name and photo. I let them know that he might be in the area and that he's potentially connected to the man who broke into your rental house. But your Dad's right. It's best if you get out of there. Whether you leave tonight or tomorrow, be careful, be aware of your surroundings."

Her father made a final plea for her to come home, and after she agreed, they said their good-byes. Barbara turned and found Griffin standing across the room, watching her.

"Apparently the guy I killed does have a business partner."

"My sister and her husband have a second home at the beach. We could go there," Griffin said.

"I don't want to involve you any more than I already have. I mean, you've been shot, and now I'm a sitting duck in your home and that puts you at risk again."

He stepped closer to her and took her hands in his. "I have this sense that you're the one always helping others. At some point you're going to have to let someone help you."

Her shoulders gave way and she realized she had been holding them close to her ears. "I just don't want you or anyone else to get hurt because of me."

He wrapped his arms around her and held her close. "Tomorrow morning we can drive to my sister's place, or we can go to the bank in Charlotte and try out that key. Either way I'll help you if you'll let me."

She exhaled hard. "Okay," she finally said.

"Have another glass of wine. I'm going to try calling Luke again." He kissed her and made his way to the back of the house.

She poured herself another glass of wine and focused on the name Agent Hernandez had given her: Ajay Ravi.

She didn't know anyone by that name and couldn't recall David ever mentioning it. He must be mad now that she had killed Elias. It seemed she had unintentionally upped the stakes when she killed him. Ajay would be more determined than ever to make sure his diamonds were returned.

A chill ran up and down her back.

BEFORE GRIFFIN COULD FINISH DIALING his cousin, his phone rang.

"Yeah, Luke—" Griffin said.

"Tell me you're on your way. Tell me you at least have your ticket. Tell me you're packed," he said.

Griffin cleared his throat. "I've run into an odd situation—"

"Oh, man, not again. Tell me you're still coming, Griff. You have no idea how much work I've put into getting this set up."

"I know, I know. And we're going to do this. I promise."

"You're bailing."

"I'm not bailing. I got shot."

"Shot?"

While Griffin told his cousin about the events of the day, he leaned around the corner and watched Barbara. He had finally met someone who wasn't just a distraction, someone he thought he could trust. That wasn't supposed to happen, not now. Long-distance relationships didn't work, he had seen that with Loralee. He still wasn't sure which choice made their relationship fall apart more—pursuing his dream or giving it up.

All he knew was that he couldn't make the same mistakes with Barbara. She was anchored to Charlotte to care for her father, so, living abroad wasn't a possibility.

Luke reaffirmed that they had worked their entire lives for this archaeological opportunity. It wouldn't come around again and Luke couldn't do this without him. Griffin had promised him that if there were a next time, that neither hell nor high water would keep him from going. He had to go. If he gave it all up again, he knew he would regret that choice for the rest of his life.

"The doctor said no swimming in lakes or streams for three weeks, and no traveling for a week. He wants to make sure an infection doesn't develop. So, I'm not bailing. Okay?"

"Sorry, man. I'm just—it's important and—listen, you take good care of yourself and I'll see you in a week," Luke said.

"I'll be there. I promise." Griffin said.

Barbara rested her head on Griffin's chest and watched the embers glow in the fireplace. His friend Mac had parked his police cruiser in the front driveway just as Griffin had said that he would. Every now and then they heard a car drive by. Each time she peeked out the side window near the door to see who it was, she saw a police car driving slowly over the dirt road. They would stop and shine a searchlight over Griffin's front yard and the surrounding area. Once, a uniformed policeman got out with his flashlight and walked around the yard. When he saw her looking out the narrow window, he waved and gave her the thumbs-up sign.

A coyote howled in the dark.

The rush of the nearby waterfall ran like white noise, lulling her into a restless sleep.

She dreamed fitful dreams of chasing someone down narrow and twisting hallways, his face just out of her sight, his fast footsteps echoing on the tiled floor. Diamonds and stars lined the walls, and when she touched them she cut her hands on their sharp edges. Blood ran over her palms and spilled onto the floor.

She rounded the corner and found David standing alone in a small room, facing her, like he waited for her. Expected her. He wore his usual navy blue shirt with the white company logo on the front pocket. "David?" she said. "You nearly got me killed."

He lifted his arms slowly, pointed a gun at her, and fired.

"No!" she screamed.

She felt the bullet hit her chest with the same sharp burn she had felt in her arm once before. She sat up with a gasp, her heart running at double speed.

"Barbara—" Griffin called.

She pressed her hand to the wound on her chest, tried to stop the bleeding, tried to stop the pain.

She turned to find Griffin sitting on the edge of the couch.

"It's alright. I think you just had a dream," he said.

She looked down and dragged her fingers over the blue

top Lillian had brought her. No blood, no wound. Her mouth was dry. "A dream."

"It's okay," he said softly and ran his hand over her back.

Her text alert sounded. She slid out of Griffin's embrace and took her phone from the coffee table. The message was from Kris:

CALL ME.

Kris never used all caps. She dialed her number and peeked out of the blinds. A hint of orange glowed from behind the mountains; the sun would be up soon.

"Barb?" Kris said.

"Yeah, what's wrong? Is Pop okay?"

Kris exhaled hard. "Last time I spoke to your dad, he had just talked to you on the phone last night. He told me he was going to the warehouse to look through the files again. I called him this morning and he didn't answer. So I went to the warehouse. The lights were on in Pop's office, and there was a note."

"What kind of note?"

"Someone's taken him. Pop's been kidnapped."

Barbara and Griffin walked into her father's home, there were three men gathered around recording equipment at the dining room table. Agent Hernandez approached them from the family room. "Barbara," he said and put his arm around her. "We're going to get him back. I promise."

Kris ran in from the kitchen, holding her swollen belly, her eyes red from crying. "Oh, Barb! I'm so sorry. I'm so sorry. I should have checked on him again last night."

"It's not your fault, it's mine. I should never have left him," Barbara said and hugged Kris tight.

She introduced Griffin to everyone, then she began asking questions about what was being done to locate her father.

"Since we're not sure where the kidnapper will call, we put recording equipment on the warehouse landline and here as well," Agent Hernandez said. "So far we've gotten this email."

He showed her a printed email with a photo attached: her dad tied to a chair with a gag in his mouth, a blindfold over his eyes, and his face badly bruised. Barbara's heart hit the floor.

The email read: Tell Barbara to give us the diamonds, and we'll make sure her father gets returned unharmed. She has 48 hours.

She pressed her palm to her forehead. "I don't have any diamonds!"

"I've replied to his email and told him as much. Also told him I'd rather talk with him over the phone and sent him my number," Agent Hernandez said.

"Pop's on medication," Barbara said. "Blood pressure and blood thinners and heart meds. He can't go without them. He's already had two heart attacks. His blood pressure is probably through the roof right now."

"Kris told us. First, I need to get the kidnapper on the phone with our hostage negotiator."

"What about money? We don't have diamonds, but how about if we offer him money in lieu of?"

Agent Hernandez looked at the floor for a painfully long moment. When he finally looked at her again he said, "We can try that, and I'll get funds from the FBI to offer them, but they may think we're keeping the diamonds from them. That could anger them. Regardless, we can't offer anything right away. Statistics don't favor a happy ending if we give in too quickly. We have to be patient, let them make their move."

Panic erupted inside of her and she pressed her hand against her chest.

"I can't do nothing," she said. "I can't just sit around and wait." She thought about the key in her purse and the bank with the fire and the fountain.

"I understand that you want to help him. But we have to

play this carefully; otherwise we won't see your father again," Agent Hernandez said.

"What if I'm able to find the diamonds?" Her words came out quickly.

"You know where they are?" he asked.

"No. But I can run around to banks and try to figure out what that key belongs to. There's one that—"

"I think we should stick with our hostage negotiator. We don't need anyone trying to be a hero." He patted her shoulder and returned his attention to the other policemen.

"It wasn't an either/or suggestion," she said under her breath as she walked away.

Griffin stood on the opposite side of the room and his head moved in a slow nod, as if he knew what she was thinking.

Kris walked up to her, her hand cradling her belly.

"Kris," Barbara whispered. "We'll be back."

"Where are you going?"

"I have a lead on the diamonds that I need to follow up on. Call me as soon as you know something."

BARBARA AND GRIFFIN reached the bank just before it opened. The fountain out front was just as she had seen on the website: streams of water circling a red hot dancing flame. The security guard unlocked the front door to the bank with a ka-chunk, and they walked inside.

When they reached the safety deposit box area, Barbara went through the same procedure as she had before, showing her license, her marriage certificate, and David's death certificate.

"Do you know the account number?" The banker

glanced quickly at Griffin and flipped her long red hair behind her shoulder.

"I don't, actually. My husband was always better at keeping track of those details." Barbara managed a smile.

"That's okay, we'll look it up. My name is Tasha and if your husband had an account here I'll be able to find it for you." She squinted at the screen, scrolling through what must have been a long list of names. "I don't see it. Could it be under another name?"

A wave of despair washed over her. Griffin slid his arm around her waist and she leaned into him for support.

She wondered if David had used the name on the passport she had found in his other safety deposit box, but she couldn't remember that name at the moment. Neither would she be able to prove that she was married to someone with that name, and therefore entitled to access their safety deposit box.

"Oh, here it is. Sorry about that. Box number 157. Here, I'll take you to it."

Tasha guided them to the small room and inserted her key into the lock chamber. Barbara held her breath and inserted her key as well. Tasha removed the small metal box and handed it to her.

When Barbara was alone with Griffin, she didn't hesitate to lift the lid. This time she hoped the diamonds were inside. They weren't.

Instead she found a crumpled piece of white notepaper, one that had been crinkled and folded so many times that it had become as soft as a piece of fabric. She imagined it had traveled miles upon miles in the safety of David's pocket or wallet.

Written in blue ink and in David's block lettering were the words:

Next to the two monumental stars that were built to stay
free.
Beneath the first window, down two, over three.

BELOW THE WORDS was a hand-drawn American flag. It was
reversed, like it flew in the opposite direction. Stars on the
upper right instead of the upper left.

"This has to be where he's hidden the diamonds." She
read the message again, and again. "Two monumental
stars," she whispered aloud. "Built to stay free. This sounds
so familiar." She wracked her memory banks. Where had
she heard these expressions before?

Griffin took the paper, read the message several times. "I
think this is the information he would have given you if he
had had time. Writing the clue out like this—he was trying
to find a way to give you the information you needed to find
the diamonds, without making it obvious to someone else
who might see it."

He ran his finger over the reversed flag. "Not sure what
this drawing means." He handed her the paper.

She folded it, put it in a side pocket of her purse. "It's a
puzzle and these are the clues. He knew how much I liked
puzzles and cryptograms. He used to buy me new ones
every...week or so." She exhaled hard, like the realization
knocked the wind out of her.

"He was getting you to practice wasn't he? He was getting
you ready in case this moment came," Griffin said.

She nodded. Paced. "Is it just me or does the phrase
'built to stay free' sound familiar?" she asked.

"It does sound familiar." Griffin looked out the windows at the top of the room like he tried to recall where he'd heard the phrase before.

She mentally revisited the stars that David had placed around the house, as well as the many discussions they had about them. Flashes of her father, cuffed and blindfolded sent worry and panic zapping through her insides like lightning bolts. She lowered her head into her hands. "Come on, think."

Several moments later she stood, closed the lid on the safety deposit box, reached for her phone. "Maybe it's a phrase everyone knows. Not just something that David said to me." She inputted the phrase into the browser.

"It reminds me of something from my childhood," Griffin said. "Something from school or from a class trip."

Before the search results fully populated on the screen, the answer came to her in the form of a memory.

She took the folded paper from her purse and put it on the table. Then she took a blank notepad and a pen from the middle of the table and began to write.

"David took me to Café Monte for brunch one Sunday morning, it's this French restaurant in Charlotte. They have these enlarged black and white photographs of the 1800s and 1900s Paris hung around the restaurant. Which of course led David to tell me about the history of the Statue of Liberty, how it was commissioned in the 1870s and arrived in America in the 1880s."

"That's it," Griffin said. "It's an old anagram."

Barbara nodded and pointed at the two phrases she had written on the paper:

Built to Stay Free
The Statue of Liberty

"The letters from the first phrase can be logically rearranged into another sensical phrase. Brilliant," Griffin said. "I remember. Eighth-grade field trip to New York City, one of the teachers showed me this."

"David used to work at the Statue of Liberty when he was a park ranger." She pulled the paper out and read the message again.

Next to the two monumental stars that were built to stay free.

Beneath the first window, down two, over three.

"Next to the two monumental stars. Monumental has two meanings—huge and commemorative. So, definitely the Statue of Liberty. Where are the stars on the statue?" She leaned over to see the images Griffin had pulled up on his phone.

"See here." He pointed to an aerial photo of the Statue of Liberty. "Look at the base of the statue, it's an eleven pointed star."

"A hendecagram," she said. "David taped a hendeca-gram to the side of the refrigerator."

"Then there's the halo she wears," he said. "A lot of people think the spikes coming out of her crown represent the seven continents. But they're the rays from the sun, which is also—"

"A star." She snapped her fingers. "David taped a graphic of the sun above the ceiling fan in the den. The sun is a star. A dying star."

"That's right." He looked at her, his expression resolute. Brave. He pressed his lips to hers, his kiss soft and yielding. "We're going to find these diamonds. And we're going to get your father back."

Strength and hope mixed in her heart and fueled her determination.

They left the bank, the sidewalk and cross streets crowded with morning traffic. Halfway to the parking garage, she stopped and looked around.

"Everything okay?" he asked.

"I have that feeling, like someone's watching us."

Griffin searched the area with a long look. He slipped his arm around her and they picked up their pace. "Come on. Let's get out of here."

16

"They called." Kris' voice was thick from crying.

Barbara's chest clenched tight with panic. "What happened?"

"The negotiator answered the phone, he was super calm. The guy on the other end just had this normal voice, no accent, but very impatient. The negotiator told him that before we handed over the diamonds, we needed proof that Pop was alive. So they posted a video of him with a time-stamp. Agent Hernandez says we can't trust it, that one of us needs to talk with him in a two-way video call. He's trying to set that up so that they have some time to track down his location. He looks like he's in bad shape."

The panic grabbed Barbara's heart and squeezed. "What did you see?"

"He seemed disoriented. Kept asking where he was and who they were, what they wanted. They said we have forty-four more hours to return the diamonds, and if they don't have them by then, they said they're going to kill him. Then they would move on to the next family member and the next, until they got what was theirs."

Barb's fingers tightened around the steering wheel, her knuckles turned white.

"I've got the plane tickets," Griffin whispered and held up his phone.

Barbara turned onto the highway and sped toward the airport. "Were they able to trace the call?"

"Yes, and Agent Hernandez just sent a bunch of police to an apartment complex off Old Concord Road. He said we shouldn't get too excited, though, because it could have been a burner phone. Or they could have been sitting in a car while they used that phone. Maybe they even tossed it afterward."

"I just came from that area."

"Did you find the diamonds?" Kris whispered.

"No. But I have another lead. I'm on my way to New York to follow through on it. Keep me posted on Pop."

AJAY RAVI BLENDED into the crowd at the airport by wearing dark jeans, a dark baseball hat, dark glasses and dark blue running shoes. There were so many garish outfits in public crowds that when someone wore dark, simple clothing, they were often overlooked.

He kept to himself. But he also kept a close watch on Barbara and her new friend, Griffin. Whatever they had found at the bank had them running, searching. Kidnapping her father had done the trick. Elias had been right about that, at least. Sometimes people just needed enough motivation to do the right thing.

He stood directly behind Barbara and Griffin at the kiosk while they printed their tickets. He could easily see the screen. Their destination? LaGuardia.

ONCE AT LAGUARDIA BARBARA and Griffin caught a cab to Battery Park. There they boarded a boat to Liberty Island. The boat rocked and chugged toward the Statue of Liberty. The cool wind whipped over the water and chilled her bare arms. She leaned into Griffin and he held her close.

She hadn't been to Liberty Island since she was in elementary school and she couldn't remember much of anything she had seen back then. She had no idea where David would have found a place to safely hide something as valuable as diamonds.

They could do this, she assured herself. If the diamonds were still there, they would find them. They had to. Because Barbara hadn't been able to stop her mother's death, or her father's heart attacks or David's murder. But she knew if she could find the diamonds, she had a real chance at saving her father's life.

She opened David's note and reread the message for the hundredth time in the last few hours. Next to the two monumental stars that were built to stay free. Beneath the first window, down two, over three. She watched the Statue of Liberty grow taller as the boat neared its port.

"What does that mean—beneath the first window, down two, over three?" she asked.

Griffin shrugged. "I'm not sure. I haven't been here in years."

They wandered up to the first floor of the statue and looked around.

Barbara studied the note and searched the area. "We have to find a window. The hiding spot is beneath the first window."

"The base of the statue—the hendecagram—is an old

fort, so there aren't going to be any windows there. Let me see the paper again," Griffin said.

"Next to the two monumental stars," she said and pointed to the first line David had written. "Next to them."

They went outside and Griffin squinted into the distance. He made a fist. "I think I know." He took her hand and they walked away from the statue, trying hard to look like any other tourist.

Barbara took stock of her surroundings, searching the crowd to make sure they weren't being followed, or watched. But there were too many people. "Where are we going?" she asked.

"Just over here." He nodded to a small, one-story house that was located across the island and behind a row of trees. A white maintenance truck was parked beside the house and a man pushed a lawnmower over the grassy lot.

"Windows," she said. There were several on at least two sides of the house that she could see.

When they got closer to the house they walked all the way around it, avoiding the man with the lawnmower and ducking below the windows just in case someone was inside.

"Which window is the first one?" she said aloud, referring to David's wording. She turned back to the statue and decided on the one closest to Lady Liberty. "This one."

Griffin turned toward the statue, then again toward the house. "Good idea."

"Down two and over three," she said. "He had to have been talking about the bricks." From the lowest part of the window she counted down two rows and over three bricks. She scraped at the mortar and bits of it began to chip away. "Try this one."

They both searched the area to make sure no one was watching.

"Wait here," Griffin said. He ducked low and crept to the maintenance truck. He returned with a small toolbox, and dug in it until he pulled out a small, serrated blade with an orange handle.

He jabbed the blade into the edges of the mortar until a strip of the sealant popped out. The brick wiggled loose and he handed it to her.

She reached into the hollow chamber and removed a black velvet bag, her knuckles scraping on the sides of the brick. Inside the bag were dozens and dozens of stones, white, sparkling, priceless. She held a few in her palm, ran her finger over them.

"Diamonds," she whispered to Griffin and handed him the bag. "He really stole them."

"They probably came from Africa," he said. "Blood diamonds out of Africa are big business. They usually go through India and then around the world."

"Ajay must have been importing them through David's business." She poured the diamonds back into the bag, wondered if David knew about the diamonds ahead of time or if he stumbled upon them by mistake.

The curtain moved in the window and Barbara gasped. A dark-haired man in a park ranger uniform rapped on the glass. "What are you two doing here?"

Griffin took Barbara by the hand and backed away from the house. He smiled gently, waved. "We were with a tour and—sorry. We got separated."

"This is a private house. You can't be here," the man yelled.

The park ranger spoke into a walkie-talkie that was attached to his uniform at the shoulder. He eyed the toolbox on the ground. "This is Eugene, I've got two young people poking around at my house, I need two officers down here to take them in for trespassing."

"Sorry!" Barbara waved and flashed her friendliest smile. "Run," she whispered to Griffin.

They ran until they reached the crowd, where Griffin guided them into the thickest flow of people. Barbara's heart pounded so hard, she was breathless. If she were stopped and searched, they would find the diamonds.

"Through here," Griffin said. He guided them to a free-standing vendor. He threw two twenty-dollar bills on the narrow counter for two NYC baseball caps and two pair of gold-rimmed sunglasses. "Put these on. Tuck your hair into the cap if you can."

They slowed their pace through the crowd, glasses on, caps pulled low. When they reached the ferry, Barbara found an isolated corner and called Agent Hernandez. Without mentioning the diamonds specifically, she told him that she had what Ajay was looking for. "They can have these, just as soon as I get my father back," she said. "Do you have his location?"

"We think he's on the west side of town. I've got police canvassing that area now. But, Barbara, we haven't gotten the live video call with your father yet. We need to have the proof that he's alive before we offer them the diamonds. We have to maintain that leverage."

"Just tell them, so they won't hurt him."

"I can't," he said. "We have to do this my way."

17

B arbara and Griffin ran from the boat landing toward the cab stand at top speed.

"Cab!" Griffin yelled and raised his hand in the air.

"Hurry," Barbara whispered under her breath. "Hurry, hurry, hurry."

"Barbara?"

She and Griffin turned. A man in dark clothing and reflective sunglasses approached them. He reached into his pocket, retrieved his wallet and showed them his photo I.D. A silver badge shone on one side and written details on the other: Charlotte Police, Detective Greg Kendall. He was tall, muscular, brown skin.

"Agent Hernandez sent me. He said you might need an escort back to Charlotte."

She backed up several steps and focused on his face.

He leaned closer to them. He stood too close for a stranger, and his smile was too deliberate to be genuine.

She recognized him.

The driver's license picture that Agent Hernandez had

sent her. Even with his glasses, the angle of his jaw gave him away. It was Ajay.

"Assuming you were able to find what you needed." His voice was even, but a forced kind of low, trying to appear authoritative.

Griffin seemed to sense that something was wrong as well and he stepped closer to her.

"Unfortunately, we didn't find them," she said. "Thank you for your offer. But right now I just need to get back home." She felt Griffin's hand pressing at the center of her back, urging her forward. She tried to step around Ajay but he blocked her.

"We really have to get home, officer. The situation is urgent and we have to be there to help," Griffin said. He guided Barbara to step around the man.

Again he blocked their path and this time he pointed a gun at them. "If you don't have them, then you won't mind if I check your bag."

Barbara didn't move. She swallowed around the tightness in her throat.

"Hand me your purse," he said.

Reluctantly, she took her purse from her shoulder. "You're Ajay," she said. "The man my husband stole from."

He did a quick double-take, like he hadn't expected to be recognized. "Give me your bag."

She shook her head. "First I need to know where my father is, then you'll get your diamonds."

He reached into his jacket pocket and pulled out a key that hung on a curled orange cord. "He's in a storage facility, waiting for you to return what's mine. You hand them over and I'll tell you where he is."

She pulled the black velvet bag from her purse and stared at the gun. "How did you find us?"

"I've been shadowing you all day—from the moment you left your father's house to your trip to the bank. I stood right behind you at the airport. You discussed LaGuardia while you printed your tickets, and I knew exactly where to go. Even managed to get on the same flight." He snatched the bag from her and Griffin lunged.

Ajay jabbed the gun in his direction, and Griffin stopped.

He opened the bag and a slow smile spread across his face. "Good work."

"What about my father?" she asked.

"I'll be in touch." He backed away, keeping the gun focused on them until he got into his car and sped away.

Barbara fished her phone from her purse and called Agent Hernandez. "We just ran into Ajay. He took the diamonds. He said my dad is in a storage facility unit. He showed me a key on one of those orange stretchy curled bands that you can put on your wrist." She thought of the westside location in Charlotte where the kidnapper's phone call had come from. "What storage facilities on the westside have orange as a part of their logo?"

"I'll look it up," he said.

After a moment, Griffin pointed to a search listing on his phone screen. "This one."

"Try the Queen's City Storage Units on Old Concord," she said.

"That's the same area where the call came from," Agent Hernandez said. "We're on our way."

The call disconnected and she looked at Griffin. "I hope we're not too late."

～

Kris stood behind the police officers who crowded the small, dingy office at Queen's City Storage Units, an outdoor facility with over five hundred storage spaces. Her ankles swelled, her back ached.

It had taken an hour and a half for Agent Hernandez to get a warrant from the judge. Now several officers stood behind the owner of the storage facility while he checked his computer records for any name that matched Ajay's or one of his companies. So far, no luck.

Agent Hernandez ran his hand over his face, his patience was gone. He motioned to four officers in the back of the room who held chain cutters at their side. "Head out. Now. This is taking too long."

"You can't cut the locks off every unit—"

"Send me a bill." Agent Hernandez stormed out of the building.

"Thank God." Kris followed them outside.

The police officers divided their efforts among the rows of storage units. Kris stood back while they went from unit to unit with the chain cutters, snapping off locks and raising doors one by one.

Kris texted Barbara: Checked three units, no sign of him yet.

Then: Opened five more, nothing.

Kris continued to text updates to help keep Barbara's mind off of worst-case scenarios. As long as there were more units to explore, there was still hope. But the police cracked lock after lock with no sign of her dad.

At the final row of storage units, Kris watched carefully, bit the skin around her nails. Their feverish pace sent metal locks clattering to the concrete. Doors rattled up. After a cursory glance and no sign of human life, they ran to the next unit.

Kris' phone rang. Barbara's name illuminated the screen, their plane must have just landed. She didn't want to answer, didn't want to give her bad news. "We're still searching, honey."

"Still?" Barbara's voice was just shy of a scream. She told Kris how Ajay had taken the diamonds, how he had probably left the country by now.

"We got him!" an officer yelled.

Kris gasped, walked as fast as she could to the open unit where the officers gathered.

"They found him, Barb. They found him," Kris said quickly. "He was locked in a unit in the middle of the lot."

"Is he okay?" Barbara cried.

Pop was slumped over and tied to a chair. Medics lifted his head, his face and neck were bruised like he'd been beaten. His eyes squinted shut against the light.

"I think he's going to be okay," Kris said. "No one else was around. Either they left when they heard us coming or whoever put him there was just going to let him die a slow death in that Godforsaken place."

One of the medics stepped away and reached for his bag.

Kris ran to Pop's side, kissed his cheek. Apologized profusely. She held his face in her hands. "Are you alright?"

He nodded. "Ajay," he whispered. "Ajay did this."

"Excuse me, ma'am," one of the medics said.

They cut the tape from his wrists and helped him on to the waiting gurney.

"They're getting into the ambulance right now. Hang on just a minute." Kris put the phone on speaker.

"Barb? Are you there?" Pop's voice was weak and scratchy.

"I'm here, Pop. I'm here," Barb said.

Kris knew that Barb must have wanted to crawl through the phone to get to him, to help him however she could.

"Oh, sweetheart," Pop said.

The medics hoisted the gurney into the ambulance and slammed the doors.

"It's me," Kris said. "They're taking him to Carolinas Medical Center."

"I'm on my way," Barb said.

18

Griffin and Barbara stood in front of the hospital. The wind picked up, blowing a cold drizzle over them.

"It's amazing that he's doing as well as he is." Barbara hunched her shoulders against the wind. "They're keeping him overnight to get him rehydrated and to get his blood pressure down. But, as long as all the blood tests come back normal, he should be able to go home in the next day or so."

"I'm glad it all worked out," he said. "Could have been much worse."

She exhaled hard. "I don't even want to think about how badly things could have gone. Listen, I owe you an enormous debt of gratitude for helping me find the bank and the diamonds. You were a huge support."

"You don't owe me anything." He shook his head.

Barbara noticed a sadness in his eyes. It was the same emotion she felt. Their short time together was coming to an end and she wasn't ready to let go. But Greece was waiting for him, his dreams, his career. There was no way she would tell him not to go. She would not get between the man and the things he needed most in life. She knew how important those things were to a person. They had been within her reach at one time, too.

"We didn't figure out what the backward flag meant," he said, his eyebrows raised in question.

She shrugged. "Might not have meant anything. We found the diamonds."

He nodded, touched his hand to her face and kissed her gently, like he tried to prolong the moment. "I know I don't have a right to ask this, not with everything you have going on here," he said. "But I want you to come with me. To Greece."

Happiness rose from deep inside and cut through all the sadness. It felt right, being with him, the idea of traveling with him. "I would love that."

He kissed her again. "But you're going to say no, aren't you?"

"I have to take care of my dad. He needs me. We've had a lot of loss in our family. My mother, David and—"

"I understand," Griffin said. "I just want you to know— that I don't want to walk away from what we've started here."

She drew her finger down the middle of his chest and detoured toward his heart, drew a circle around it. "I could visit."

His lips flattened into a line and he nodded.

She knew what he was thinking, that long-distance relationships didn't work. In their case she wasn't convinced that he was wrong. It didn't seem possible to go from knowing one another for just a few days to a long-distance relationship and have that even remotely work.

"I don't want to get in the way of you and your family. It's just that—life is short. And it doesn't always turn out the way we plan. So when the right thing comes along, when the stars finally align in such a way that put your dreams within reach, I think you have to go for it. And I—I went for it. If I hadn't, I know I would have regretted that for the rest of my life." He cradled her head in his hand. "I don't do regrets anymore."

He kissed her again, a good-bye kiss this time, and it nearly broke her heart.

19

B arbara sat in the courtyard behind her condo. She let the soft winds caress her skin, let it run its fine fingers through her hair. As she had so often done over the last year and a half, she closed her eyes and tried to pretend that the crows calling in the distance were seagulls, that she was on the beach in Greece. That the rustle of the breeze through the trees was the deep blue ocean rolling onto the white sand.

But this time it didn't work. She knew why. Before David died, she had it in the back of her mind that she would actually go to Greece. Now, she couldn't bring herself to visit the country. Not now that Griffin was there, not now that she knew what she was missing.

Their connection was meant for something beautiful, something long-lasting. It would hurt too much to either go and miss out on seeing him altogether, or to see him for just a few days—knowing they couldn't have anything more.

Her heart ached at the thought of him. It seemed unreasonable for her to miss someone she hadn't known that long. But he had opened a door for her, one that made her want to live again, one that made her realize how she hadn't lived in a very long time.

She would have thought the connection they shared would have given her the lasting sense of direction she wanted to rebuild her life. But it still evaded her.

Kris had called earlier and said that Stephen was coming home. The army was letting him take his unused leave time to end his tour early, so he could be home for the birth of his daughter.

"My life is about to be completely different—with a husband and a baby in the house!" Kris had said. "You're going to have to rescue me once a week, girls' night out. Okay?"

Barbara was happy for her. Dreams like that should come true.

She'd like to think that Stephen would help with Pop, but he and their father had never gotten along. They were too much alike. Both of them were too headstrong and obstinate.

She went inside and scanned the quiet home that had once been so full of life. She had spent more than enough time mourning the loss of her dreams, the loss of David and the child they would never have together. But she hadn't spent much time, if any, dismantling the framework of those dreams. She still wasn't sure how she was ever going to effectively move on with her life. She did know that she had to get rid of the condo.

She pulled David's note from her pocket, the one with the handwritten clues. She stared at the backward flag. They had found the diamonds, so it was possible that the flag didn't mean anything. Just a patriotic symbol that somehow tied into the Statue of Liberty.

She stared at the image. It had been drawn several lines

below the clues.

She shook her head.

David was specific, deliberate. Everything he did had a purpose.

This had to mean something.

She folded the paper, put it in her pocket and returned her attention to the condo. There wasn't much left to do. Kris had handled most of the packing while Barbara had been in Brevard. She had removed most of the stars. There were just a few more that were too high for Kris to get to.

Barbara went upstairs and looked at all the stars that David had affixed to the upper walls and ceiling of what they thought would be their child's nursery. Kris had said that the house would show better if all their personal touches were gone. So Barbara dragged a ladder from the hallway to the edge of the room and started peeling.

The front door slammed on the level below. "Barbara?"

"Up here, Pop!" she called.

The adhesive was thick and gummy. Gluey.. It was no wonder that Kris couldn't get those removed, too sticky and too much of a balancing act. She took a knife from the toolbox and jiggled it in between the wall and the soft, decorative star. Bits of the sheetrock hit her in the face.

"Where?" her father called, his footsteps trudging up the squeaky stairs.

"In here," she said and wiped plaster remnants out of her eye.

"Oh, wow. You want some help?"

"No, I got it." She turned and looked at him. "You're getting your color back, and those bruises are fading. You're putting the arnica gel on them like I showed you?"

"No," he said, grinning wide.

She rolled her eyes. "What's the point of people helping you if you aren't going to follow direction?"

"I've never been all that good at following orders. I did just get a text from Agent Hernandez. A guy in London approached an upscale jeweler on Hatton Garden, their diamond district. He tried to cash in a bunch of diamonds. The jeweler called the authorities while he was there, said it was such a large quantity of jewels, something didn't seem right."

"Ajay?" she asked, hoping they caught him.

"They sent a photo from the store security camera."

She climbed down the ladder and Pop showed her a photo on his phone screen.

That face. Her blood boiled with fury. She gripped the knife tight, wanted to jab it in Ajay's throat.

"Agent Hernandez had an APB and an APW on him, so this information made it back to him." Pop swiped the photo and showed her his screen again. "They got him, sweetheart. They moved fast and they arrested him."

She looked at her father's phone again and saw a photo of Ajay wearing orange and standing against a gray background. There was no sign of the smug look she'd last seen on his face.

"Thank God." She released her grip on the knife.

"If they extradite him back to the U.S. I'm going to enjoy testifying against him." Her father stretched his jaw like it was still sore.

"Me, too," she said. They exchanged a look, one that said they were glad it was all behind them.

"I could use a drink. How about you?" she said.

He nodded. "I'm in."

They went downstairs to the kitchen. She opened one of the boxes that Kris left on the countertop, found two shot glasses and a bottle of vodka. She filled them. They faced one another, held the glasses up in a toast.

"What shall we drink to?" he asked.

She shook her head. "Something. The end of a horrible mess? I don't know."

"How about new arrangements?" her father suggested.

She wanted to roll her eyes. She didn't. There weren't any new arrangements that she was excited about right now. "Sure."

Their glasses clinked together and they each drank the vodka in one gulp. They returned the shot glasses on the counter at the same time.

Her father looked at her for a long moment, a quiet smile on his lips. "It's going to be okay."

She nodded again. He had been saying that to her for almost two years now. "Follow me back upstairs? I need to get some final clean up done in the—in that bedroom."

"Listen, sweet pea. I've been thinking," her father said.

"Thinking about what?" She heard the irritation creep into her voice and she silently chastised herself. It wasn't right for her to be frustrated with him. She was just disappointed about Griffin. She would get over him, she would heal. Life moved on.

"I think we need to work out a new arrangement," he said.

"What kind of new arrangement?" She began to climb the second set of stairs and her father gently grabbed her arm.

"You've done so much for me since your mother died. I couldn't have gotten through it without you. You've been my rock."

She turned, faced him on the landing. He had a renewed strength such that the blue in his eyes appeared electric.

Even youthful.

"Same goes for you, Pop. Not sure how I would have gotten through David's death without you." Something hit her funny about hearing her former husband's name aloud. There was a finality to it. As if in that very moment, her life with him moved further into the past. Relegated to faraway memories like old pictures and things to be discussed at the Thanksgiving dinner table.

He took her hands in his. "I think I may have done you a disservice. You're young, honey, and—"

"Pop, you've been through two heart attacks and you lost your wife. That's too much for one person and there's no way I wouldn't have been there for you."

"See, that's one of the reasons I appreciate you so much. You give beyond measure. But—"

"Pop, don't."

"No—Barb. Hear me out. I think we've gotten into a pattern, and maybe not a healthy one. When your mother died and after the heart attacks, I thought my life was over. You've been so attentive, but I've leaned on you too much. You're living more like you're my age instead of your own. You have a lot of life ahead of you. You need to go live it."

She opened her mouth to object and he gestured for her to wait.

"I would enjoy a little more independence in my life these days. Being kidnapped and held in that dark storage unit made me realize that I'm not ready for my life to be over. I have a son coming home and a grandchild to welcome into the world. I need to lighten up and live the life I have left.

"I love you, and I appreciate everything you've done for me. But I don't want you to sit on the sidelines of life to take care of me. Your mother and I saved well, I can hire companion care if things get that bad. Stephen might step up to the plate and help now and then, if I need him to. Becoming a dad might soften him."

She gave him a wide-eyed look.

He said, "I'll try to be more agreeable with him, too. Look, I don't know much about this Griffin character, but I would just say that you're smart and intuitive. If you think he's a good guy, then maybe you should take a chance on him."

"I'm not going to leave you to travel halfway around the world with someone I hardly know." Her heart clenched like it reached for a dream and missed.

"You have a gift for reading people. If you got a good read on him, you should trust that." His blue eyes, clear and strong, focused intently on her.

"Well, my instincts don't always tell me anything. I couldn't read David."

"I think I may be able to shed some light on that." Her dad reached into his back pocket and handed her a folded piece of paper.

"When the police were here gathering fingerprints on the night of the break-in, they found a set throughout the house that didn't belong to anyone we knew, including some on the door to the firewall. I had Agent Hernandez run a search on them, to see what might come up."

Barbara opened the paper and it shook in her hands. There was a picture of David's face on a California driver's license.

"I didn't get the report until this morning. Turns out that David Silver wasn't his real name. His real name was Adam Drucker."

She read the name aloud, associated it with the man she knew as her former husband: "Adam." He looked like an

Adam. She'd known that David had always kept something from her. She hadn't been able to put her finger on what it was.

Her heart thumped heavy and hard and made her breathless.

"I had a hunch that if he had stolen this time, it probably wasn't the first time," her dad said. "So I had Agent Hernandez do some digging and he discovered that David had worked for another import/export business in Los Angeles under his real name. That business was investigated in a case a few years back for—guess what?"

"Diamond smuggling," she said softly.

"Bingo." He pointed his finger in her direction. "My guess is that David somehow saw how easy it was to get away with taking a few diamonds and decided to replicate that business on the opposite coast. He was smart to do it under a fake name the second time around. Unfortunately, he got caught."

Barbara thought of her history with cancer, and the photo of David and his mother that he always kept in his pocket. "He always said he was going to make darn sure he could take care of his family. No matter what life threw at them."

She and her father looked at one another for a long moment. He was still her protector. She was still his supporter. They were still a team.

"How would he have been able to replicate that business?" she asked.

"All of these smuggling rings operate legitimate businesses on the surface. I'm sure he left Los Angeles with their contact information. He probably solicited them as an honest import/export business looking to gain new customers. Only he knew their businesses were a cover for smuggling gems. Once they signed with him, all he had to do was wait for the shipments to roll in. Then, he would search the crates and their contents to figure out where diamonds were hidden. He would only have to take one diamond now and then to make a small fortune."

She shook her head in amazement. "I don't know why he didn't just trade the diamonds in for cash."

"He must have traded a few in order to pay off the medical bills. Beyond that, he was probably playing it safe. Cash is a lot harder to hide than diamonds. That's why the smuggling rings are such big business, diamonds are easy to hide."

"That still doesn't tell me why I couldn't get a read on him."

"I don't think it's all that complicated. You knew he was hiding something—"

"I lived with the man, I should have known something. I should have had a clue."

Her father shrugged. "You loved him. Love can create a lens. We're all like that to some extent. When we love someone we want to see the best in them, so we overlook things. Sometimes important things. It's not intentional."

She stood on the stairs with her father, crossed her arms, covered her mouth with her hand.

"You need to let yourself off the hook," he said.

Her eyes filled with tears.

"No matter how good you are at seeing things that most people don't, you're not going to see everything. Not all the time anyway."

He opened his arms and gathered her into a big bear hug. His spearmint aftershave was strong and familiar and gave her comfort.

She pulled away and noticed his smile, full of love and pride for her. It was funny how much that still meant to her.

"Another drink?" he asked.

She snickered. "No. But I do think I'll sit down for a minute."

They sat on the stairs, glanced around the lower floor, talked a bit about what to do next.

"Oh." She dug into her pocket and retrieved David's note of clues, showed the drawing of the flag to her father. He had been in the army, maybe he would know what it meant. "This may not mean anything, but what does it signify when the flag is shown flying backward?"

Her father took the paper and studied the drawing.

"I searched but it seems there are several explanations, none of which are meaningful in terms of a clue," she said.

"The image reversal comes from the days when men carried flags into battle. The stars are always closest to the pole, where the flag is attached. So a flag bearer rushing into the fray leads with the stars. Nowadays, when soldiers have the flag patch on both shoulders of the uniform, the image has to be reversed on one sleeve, the right sleeve. Otherwise you're leading with stripes and not stars. Stripes first would give the appearance that you're retreating."

She had seen a similar description online, but it didn't mean anything to her as it related to David. "Maybe David drew the flag as an encouragement, maybe he was just saying to charge ahead or something like that."

"Could be," Pop said with a shrug. "I've also heard it said that the field of stars has to be positioned closest to the wearer's heart and that's part of the reason for the reversal."

A sense of awareness jolted inside of her. "Heart?" she whispered.

"Yeah," he said in a light tone. He drew an imaginary line from his upper arm to his chest.

"Heart. You're carrying my heart. You're carrying our heart." She put her hand over her belly.

Pop narrowed his eyes. "Hmm?"

"Something David used to say when I was pregnant." She stood, looked around the first floor then directed her attention up the stairs. "Heart."

She dashed to the second level and headed straight for the nursery.

Pop was close behind her.

Barb scanned the ceiling and upper part of the room. "Stars close to the heart." She remembered the evenings when David sequestered himself in the nursery to glue the glow-in-the-dark stars to the upper wall and ceiling in the design of specific constellations. "When I was pregnant he used to say I was carrying his heart, carrying our heart. These are the stars close to our heart."

Pop left the room, returned with a chair. He climbed on it with the knife and scraped at one of the stars on the wall until it peeled away. He looked at the wall surface and then the underside of the star, showed Barbara. "Nothing there."

Her heart sank. "Try again."

He slid the knife under another star and stripped it from the wall. He shook his head. "Still nothing."

"This has to be it." She climbed to the top of the ladder, reached for one of the stars that David had affixed to the ceiling. She grabbed one of its legs, tugged hard. It finally ripped from the ceiling with a jerk, causing her to lose her balance, sending the star into the long shag carpet.

Her father reached for the lower half of the ladder and steadied her.

"You okay?" he asked.

"Yeah, I just want to take a look at that star."

She climbed down, and together they dug through the long, thick strands of the cream-colored carpet. Her index finger hit something sharp. She picked it up, held it in her open palm.

"Pop—" she whispered.

They each knelt, facing one another.

Her father took the diamond from her hand, held it to the light.

"It's huge," she said. "Every bit as big as the ones we found in New York."

They both looked up at the same time, stared at all the other stars affixed to the ceiling.

Barb scurried up the ladder while Pop held it firm.

"Take the knife," he said.

One by one she removed the stars from the ceiling. Behind nearly every one, stuck on the adhesive, was a large, clear diamond. Fifty diamonds in all.

"He only put diamonds behind the stars on the ceiling, the ones that were hardest to reach," Pop said.

Barb ran her fingers over the sparkling collection, dumbfounded over their size. "These have to be worth what —twenty thousand each?"

"I'd say more like fifty thousand each." Her father inspected one of the diamonds.

"That's three million dollars!" She slapped her hand to her forehead. "Why would David plant diamonds here and at the Statue of Liberty?"

The answer came to her as soon as the question left her lips. "Plan B," she and her father said together.

"David always had a plan B," her father said.

"Sometimes a plan C, as well," she said.

"I would bet he had the diamonds hidden here in the

house or maybe at the warehouse until he thought they'd caught on to him. Then he moved them. Obviously he kept some here, knowing you would be the only one to find them if anything happened to him."

Barbara nodded. "Do we turn these in to Agent Hernandez?"

Her father picked up a diamond and placed it into her palm, folded her fingers over it. "Keep them."

"Are you serious?"

"Take them for the fresh start that David, or Adam, would have wanted you to have. The police already think Ajay has the entire stash. No sense in these collecting dust in a warehouse somewhere. You keep 'em. Start that spa business you've wanted for so long. You deserve a break for a change."

She held the diamond to her chest in a closed fist and thought about what to do next.

———————

20

Griffin stood at the roped edge of what looked to be the ancient Minoan settlement that he and so many others had searched for over the years. Luke stood under the white tent, holding a stack of surveys and maps. He instructed a team of young archaeologists as to how the dig would progress.

Griffin rubbed at the ache in his chest, the one that wouldn't let go. He wondered about romantic relationships and if they could ever be truly happy for both people involved. He had watched his mother stay with his father because she thought it was best for the family, regardless of the cost to her. Then he watched her shrivel and nearly die under the weight of that obligation.

He had given up his archaeological work for Loralee, thinking that was what he needed to do to make her happy —for them to be happy. But that hadn't been enough for either of them.

Two people had to want the same things in order for a relationship to work. Sacrifice was necessary and important, but their goals had to be aligned, or at least complimentary.

Of course, love and trust had to be at the center of it all. He learned the hard way how to trust what was right for him. In relationships, it had taken him time to learn that he couldn't override that small, wise voice.

He had traveled halfway around the world to accomplish his lifelong dream of making a significant discovery. He had left Barbara to her own decisions.

There would be plenty of work, and assuming they found the lost city, accolades. Money would follow, as would prestige, and offers to lead other expeditions. It was everything he ever wanted.

He adjusted his hat to block the afternoon sun and stared at the sapphire-colored sea that stretched toward infinity. He turned his face toward the sky so bright and cloudless that it didn't look real. And yet none of its beauty touched his soul.

Luke walked toward him. Rock and dirt crunched beneath his work boots. "Good progress so far." He patted Griffin on the shoulder.

"Yeah, I'm really pleased. Listen, I'm going to head out of town for the weekend."

"Where are you going?" Luke asked.

"I'll be back on Monday."

THE YELLOW MERCEDES cab drove too fast along the narrow cobblestone streets. Barbara fumbled through her purse, trying to find her sunglasses and found the folded receipt instead. She opened up the letter-sized paper and examined the details, feeling a sense of pride.

She'd never pegged her father as someone who would help her sell stolen diamonds, but he did just that. He drove to South Carolina and sold one diamond to a small jeweler who was thrilled to get it. She and her father stuffed the cash in a bank safety deposit box where they'd never done business before and decided they needed to learn more about Swiss bank accounts.

Since the hiding place had worked so well the first time, they bought a new set of self-adhesive, glow-in-the-dark stars. This time they glued them to the ceiling in her father's attic. They figured Miller, Pop's beloved and fierce German Shepard, might have discouraged Ajay and Elias from going near the house in the weeks and months previous.

As a plan B, they put a few of the diamonds in a separate safety deposit box with yet another bank.

The receipt she held was from an anonymous cash donation she made to The American Cancer Society. She would make many more over the coming years. Always anonymous because she knew she had to be careful about her expenditures. She couldn't suddenly change her lifestyle without drawing suspicion. If Agent Hernandez noticed, the FBI would snoop.

When her phone rang, she answered right away.

"Hey Pop, everything okay?"

"Everything's great, sweetheart. Just checking on you."

"I'm good. Really good." She wanted to ask him a slew of questions about his medicines and his exercise and his diet, but she couldn't. She had to try to stick to their pact.

He had agreed to take care of himself according to doctors' orders, and she had to let him be accountable for that. In turn, she had promised to take care of herself, too. That meant no more discounting her instincts. At all. Especially when it came to her own self-care.

Pop insisted she unpack all of her travel wish books and plan and book a trip. He made her put her business plan on paper, the one she had in her head for the new spa she had always wanted to run.

"Have you gotten to the hotel yet?" he asked.

"Almost."

"Good. Well, I've got to scoot, I have a date tonight. Enjoy your trip to Greece—"

"Wait—a date?"

"Kris' mom is still here helping her with the baby. I'm taking her out to dinner tonight."

Barbara's mouth fell open. No words came out.

"What?"

"Nothing. That's just—that's great."

Barbara touched the smile that pulled the corners of her lips. Her father was happy. He really was ready to live again.

Excitement bubbled inside of her—she was ready to live, too. It had taken her some time to trust again. Funny how trust and her internal compass were so closely linked.

The key hadn't been about trusting her instincts like she had originally thought. It hadn't been about forgiving David, although that was part of it. She hadn't agreed with his choices but she understood why he made them.

Moving forward meant she had to trust guidance however it came to her. She hadn't been wrong about David. She had seen that something was amiss. That he was lying. Hiding.

She knew that when she could accept what she saw, it was easier to make good choices. If she spent too much time doubting or just wishing the information could be different, she could lose herself.

The cab screeched to a halt and Barbara braced herself on the seat in front of her. The cab driver shook his fist and yelled in Greek at the man he almost ran over.

"Goodness—" She stared at him. She hopped out of the

back seat and told the driver she needed her bag from the trunk.

"You're here," she said.

"I'm here," Griffin said, breathless.

A moment hung between them and then he framed her face with his hands. He kissed her long and slow and she lost track of everything—where she was, what she was doing. It felt like they were meant to be, like that had never been a question, like they had never been apart.

When he finally stepped back, his eyes held tears. "I wasn't sure I would see you again."

"I was afraid I might not see you again, either."

He took her by the hand and led her inside the hotel, then to the terrace that overlooked the Mediterranean Sea. They dined on grilled lamb, vegetables and freshly made pita bread. They toasted with champagne and she listened with excitement while Griffin discussed his archaeological project.

The waiter cleared their plates/ She grinned and pointed to Griffin's overnight bag that had a white sleeve hanging out of the zipper. "Looks like you packed in a hurry."

He nodded slowly. "I was coming to see you. I couldn't wait another minute."

"What about the excavation?"

He shrugged. "Being with you, holding you, sharing this with you, it's all I could think about. I needed to see you. I was hoping we could find a way to make it work."

"I'd like that," she said.

They parked her luggage behind the front desk in the lobby. Griffin reached into his zippered bag and removed a flat, white box, held it behind his back. Then he gave the clerk his bag to hold as well.

"Whatcha got there?" she grinned and nodded toward his hidden hand.

Griffin winked, ushered her outside and hailed a cab. He gave the driver directions to the dig site, which wasn't that far away.

They arrived at the site, and they walked to the edge of the property. The sea sparkled with light from the afternoon sun and Barbara marveled at the beauty. It looked like a dream, a movie, a magazine cover.

Griffin handed her the white box. "Open it," he said with a soft look in his eyes.

Inside was a beautiful yellow gold necklace with emerald, garnet, and carnelian stones. "We've found quite a few pieces of ancient jewelry at this site. This one reminded me of you. I took a photo and had this replica made for you."

She held the necklace to her chest and he fastened it at the back of her neck. Her fingers traced the smooth stones and the gold that was cool to the touch. "It's gorgeous."

He gave her a tour of the site and told her all about their progress and their plans.

It wasn't even her project, but she was enthralled with the idea that Griffin's work would soon reveal an ancient civilization.

They climbed back into the cab and Griffin had the driver drop them at the city center. Griffin narrated the history of the area and they strolled hand-in-hand along cobbled streets, past small storefronts, then made their way back to the hotel.

"How long can you stay?" he asked.

"As it turns out, my dad has a new lease on life these days. He's energized and taking care of himself. He said it was time we both started living again. So, I'm here in Greece, where I've wanted to be for a long time. My schedule is a little open-ended right now."

"That's good news," he said. "I know Greece pretty well, I could show you some other areas if you like."

"Oh yeah?"

"Yeah," he said and kissed her again. "Listen, I remember what I said about long-distance relationships. But I'll fly back and forth, I'll take time off, I'll do whatever it takes to give this a real chance. What we have here is different, it's special. In fact, there isn't anything I wouldn't do to see this through."

She checked in at the front desk and they gathered their bags. Griffin ordered a bottle of wine. He guided her along the narrow and steep outdoor path that led to his hotel rooms.

The waves crashed hard onto the shore far below and the seabirds called from the air. The courtyard from her old condo seemed so far away, like another world. One whose door had closed to her forever.

They sat on the picturesque veranda outside of his suite. He poured the wine. They held hands and took in the extraordinary view.

She caught him looking at her and she ran her hand along the outline of his face. Some smaller part of her thought it was too soon to feel the way she did. Definitely too soon to tell him about it. But the bigger part of her, the happier part, the part of her that had grown the most in the last few weeks decided differently. "I love you," she said.

His lips broadened slowly, until they formed a wide, honest grin. "I love you, too."

She closed the distance by half and met him in a kiss. She relaxed into the goodness she had sensed about him from the beginning, not at all able to explain the peace that welled up inside of her. But she settled into it all the same, trusting the insights she had gathered thus far. And let go.

She felt alive.

"Beautiful," he said, his lips against hers.

He pulled her into an embrace. She slid her hands over the iron-solid curves of his back. Her inexplicable feelings for him nearly swallowed her whole.

The talked and drank wine on the veranda until thousands of stars scattered across the dark sky. Waves crashed in the thick black of the night.

Like cold smoke leaving the dying embers of an old fire, her memories of death and loneliness swirled into the shadows. She finally remembered what it was like to be herself again. She finally remembered that she had survived.

LATER THEY WALKED hand-in-hand along the beach, he asked her who was taking care of her condo.

"No one." She smiled.

"Oh?"

"Yeah. Sold my condo. I'm as free as the birds." The tide ran over her bare feet and she dug her toes into the wet sand, enjoying the sensation.

"Did you pack a bathing suit in that bag of yours?" His lips found her neck and her toes curled.

"I did pack a bathing suit."

Griffin pulled away, gestured to the sky.

"It's full moon tonight, we could go swimming."

"I love swimming under a full moon."

"I know." Griffin wrapped his arm around her waist. His hand, wide and capably strong, pressed against her hip. She leaned into him, enjoying the comfort of his solid warmth.

The frothy white edges of the cool water washed over their pale feet. Her need to question and doubt settled, and was replaced by a peaceful acceptance of what was.

"Good. Then it's a date," he said.

"It's a date," she said.

FORCED PERSPECTIVE PROLOGUE

Mosquitoes buzzed close to our ears, fed on our thin arms and legs. The wide duct tape around our wrists prevented us from slapping the bugs. We still wore the same pajama shorts and tanks that we put on six nights ago. The horrible man with the black front tooth stared at us, the one who took us from our bunk beds in the middle of the night, the one who stank like rotting meat.

I knew there was something wrong with him from the first time I saw him at the house. I spoke up about it, several times. But Dad said I was jumping to conclusions again, being overreactive, being judgmental. He said the man was harmless, that he needed some work to get back on his feet, that we should help.

But the way he looked at Catherine and me when no one was around, like we were thickly-iced cupcakes prepared just for him, made us think differently. That's the way it was with us. We were connected. Not all twins were that way, but I felt what she felt and vice versa. We were two sides of the same coin. Two versions of the same person. And we were afraid.

We'd spent the last few days in the basement of the big house, cameras mounted in the upper corners. Other girls came in, but when they left we never saw them again. When we left, three other girls remained. The space was divided by bars like a jail. Like cages. Each small cage had one dirty mattress on the floor and a metal bucket in the corner. No one heard our screams. Or if they did, they didn't care.

The man with the black tooth visited our cell twice a day. Each time he brought a small meal. Sometimes he emptied the buckets. Because of Catherine's and my food allergies we hadn't eaten much and we were weak.

He said the same thing each time we saw him, his words heavily flavored with his Spanish accent. "Your father pay ransom. You go home."

On this particular night they moved us to the outside patio area. Just us. The other girls were still down there. Trapped. I was not encouraged when they didn't replace our blindfolds. It was a bad sign.

The house was enormous, and busy. When they led us through the upstairs, we saw men chopping and weighing mounds of white powder and putting it into small plastic bags.

No one gave us more than a passing glance. Like it wasn't unusual to see two skinny, twelve-year-old girls in dirty pajamas. Like kidnapping was part of the family business.

Maybe it was.

The black-toothed man tipped my chin, then looked at my sister, my identical twin. "Harper?" he asked, not sure who was who. No one from their family got our names right, and the only name they seemed to remember was mine. We never corrected them. He called Catherine his "special treat" and he rubbed her arm. He didn't think we understood him because he spoke in Spanish. He didn't know that our school taught Spanish to every student, beginning in kindergarten. Six years of studying one language went a long way.

He dragged his finger down Catherine's neck and along her collar bone, then he unbuckled his belt with his other hand, almost unconsciously. His smile was greasy and hungry and we knew he wanted to do something awful.

In broken English he said the ransom had been paid and that we were going home as soon as the boat came back. But neither Catherine nor I believed him because we'd seen it all—the drugs, their faces. We could see the distant city lights of Miami so we could reasonably figure out where on the coast this compound was located. Why would they let us leave now?

Several women, wives and mothers we guessed, stood nearby, watching children play on the dock and in the nearby yard. Boys and girls laughed and jumped and ran around in the grass, catching fireflies in mason jars, playing tag. Like we weren't even there. Like it was just another summer night. Like two young girls tied up wasn't uncommon at their house.

Maybe it wasn't.

A white boat pulled up to the dock, and the driver cut the motor.

The man with the black tooth watched while the driver lassoed the rope around a wooden post. Then he walked toward the edge of the marsh, fiddled with his trousers like he was unbuttoning and unzipping.

The driver of the white boat walked toward us carrying three blue duffel bags that were stuffed full. We assumed they were full of cash. The driver was short, round, and wore a black button-down shirt. His black jeans were so tight he nearly waddled. In Spanish he yelled to the black-toothed man that the alligators would take revenge on him for peeing in their water. Then he held up the duffels and said, still in Spanish, to wait until it was completely dark, then put us in the boat and drive to a nearby mangrove swamp—where the alligators would devour our bodies.

The black-toothed man responded that he would. Right after he got his fair share.

"Do it on the boat!" the man with the duffels barked and went inside the house. He didn't look at us when he passed by. He didn't think we understood what he said.

The solemn expression that fell over Catherine's face told me she knew what I was thinking. Twins just knew.

"Boat," I whispered. "As fast as you can. Take care of the rope and start the engine. I'll be right there." I was the impulsive one, the one who leaped first and asked questions later. I'd always thought it was a sign of bravery.

"What about a key?" Catherine was the one who thought everything through ahead of time. I'd always thought she played it too safe.

"He wasn't carrying one. It's probably still in the ignition." This was only a guess. But our parents owned a boat, and the only time they could find the key was when they left it in the ignition. So they usually did.

"What if they catch us?" Catherine's eyes filled with tears, her bottom lip quivered. Normally I deferred to her because my act-first-think-later approach often landed me in trouble. And she was the oldest. Only by three minutes, but she was accustomed to leading the way, being in charge, having the final say.

The joke in our family was that I resented being second. That I was always coming up from behind, fighting my way forward like a half-crazed bull. Too feisty for my own good. But tonight we had to do things my way, because there was no time to sit around and weigh rational options.

"Then we'll go down fighting. This is our only chance," I whispered.

Her worry lines told me she had lots of unanswered questions. Finally she nodded, once and quick. She ran to the empty boat, wrists still bound together in front of her. At the last second the little boys playing on the dock heard her footsteps and they moved out of the way.

The fast, spinning sensation in my chest, the feeling I always had before I sprang into action, told me it was now or never. I ran across the grass, toward the black-toothed man with my taped wrists and arms stretched in front. I shoved him hard from behind and he fell face-first into the salt-water marsh. I didn't wait to see what happened next, but the violent splashing told me that the alligators didn't give him time enough to scream.

When I reached the dock there was a boy running toward the boat, ahead of me and behind Catherine. He was tall, probably the same age as us. Maybe older. I couldn't let him get to her. I couldn't let him stop us.

She started the engine and I picked up speed.

The tall boy waved his arms, yelled for her to stop. I heard the women screaming behind me. "Matthew!"

I caught up to him, kicked one of his feet behind the other and he fell onto the dock with a thud. I leaped over him, took two steps and sprang toward the untethered and drifting boat, screaming when I was mid-air.

I slammed into the side of the boat and clung tight. "Go!"

Several children gathered on the deck, screaming, pointing, waving.

I threw one leg over the side and scrambled into the boat.

"Matthew!" I heard a woman scream, louder this time.

I stood, unsteady, and watched the tall boy stand upright. He ran to the end of the dock. Blood poured from his nose and mouth and he screamed, "Stop!"

Several men ran out of the house, waving guns.

I grabbed the wheel and the silver handle, opened the throttle. The boat engine roared, the front end tipped up. We held on and crouched low while I made a U-turn and steered the boat toward the distant glow of Miami's city lights.

Gunshots fired and we ducked.

Most of the men ran around to the other side of the house and I knew they were coming after us.

More gunshots fired.

"Did they get you?" I yelled over the noise of the engine.

"I'm okay," Catherine said weakly.

I kept my hands tight on the silver wheel, my wrists still taped together. We bounced over the waves and the door to the cabin swung open and shut again.

I silently thanked my father for all the times he let us drive his boat. We'd never driven at high speed before, but we both knew the basics.

"Can you find some scissors?" I nodded to the compartments below the steering wheel. "Something to cut the tape?"

"Yeah." Her voice was thin. It took her a minute to move.

I was scared to take my eyes off of the water ahead of us. I needed to get us all the way into the city where there were onlookers, witnesses, anyone who could help.

I turned for a quick glance behind us, and I couldn't see the compound. But I did see one round light on the water. A boat light. I knew it was them; I knew they were following us.

I also knew that at the edge of the city there were restaurants with docks over the water. Neither of us had ever parked a boat before. But I thought if I could get us close, and if we made a commotion, someone would see us. Someone would help.

The last of the sun's light faded, and speeding through the dark kept my heart in my throat. But the idea of being caught and fed to alligators kept me driving fast.

"Do you see a radio anywhere?" I asked and did a quick search around me. The boat tipped and slammed over waves and we fought hard to keep our balance. The cabin door opened with the boat's motion.

"There's a boy!" she said.

"A what?"

"There's a boy in the cabin! He's like, five or something!"

She took the wheel and slowed the speed.

"Not so slow!" I yelled and pointed to the light behind us that looked like an oncoming train.

I ducked my head inside the cabin and saw a small boy sitting on a narrow striped couch attached to the wall. He had dark hair, brown skin and eyes, and he looked like a miniature version of nearly every man we'd seen on the compound. He wore a red T-shirt, blue shorts and a frightened expression.

I returned to the wheel, shutting the cabin door behind me. My gut tightened, like a bucket of ice hit my insides. I pushed the silver handle forward.

"It's too fast!" she yelled over the noise of the engine and the wind.

"They're coming after *him*!" I increased the speed again and we fell to the floor of the boat.

She stood and screamed, "Slow down!"

Adrenaline sped through my veins, my heart slammed against my ribs. I grabbed the wheel again. My feet left the boat floor each time we hit the top of a wave. A violent jolt nearly pitched us into the ocean.

Suddenly I realized all the things I didn't know about driving a boat.

Catherine shoved me out of the way and slowed the speed. She didn't say anything but she pointed a finger close to my face, telling me not to cross her.

After a moment the light that was following us got so close I could make out the boat. It was white with no roof or shade and there were several men pointing in our direction. The Miami city lights were also bigger, closer and brighter, and I was looking for something familiar. Some place to pull over.

Our Dad loved taking us out on his boat for evening rides, then docking at a seaside restaurant for dinner. Surely one of those restaurants was coming up soon.

If it were daytime, if the sun were high in the sky, the ocean would be flooded with sailboats, yachts, motorboats of all kinds. But at night there were none.

I looked at the closed cabin door and my mind galloped like a wild horse. I thought about how frightened that poor boy must be. Certainly every bit as frightened as we were when we were taken.

"We're going to make it!" Catherine gripped my arm, pointed straight ahead. A neon blue pelican came into view like a beacon. "It's Rusty! Rusty the pelican! Go left! Go left!"

The giant bird was a sign that sat on top of Rusty's Oceanfront Restaurant. We'd docked and eaten there at least twenty times with our parents. She jumped up and down in tiny hops. I wanted to be just as happy but something bothered me. Something I couldn't quite figure out.

I looked behind us. The singular light was so close I recognized the four men in the boat. They veered to the left. It looked like they were trying to pull alongside us.

Gunfire popped like loud fireworks and we ducked. I steered to the right, away from the restaurant.

Catherine grabbed my arm, tugging it away from the wheel. "What are you doing?! Go that way!"

I shoved her away, pointing to the boat that followed us. "Too close!"

She turned the wheel toward the neon bird. Toward the floodlights outside the restaurant that shone on the dark water.

"Just get close! I'll blow the horn, scream and wave! Someone will see us! Someone will send help!" Catherine yelled over the engine.

With everything about to work for us I couldn't figure why something awful still nagged at me.

I glanced at the cabin door that was shut, and realized that even after we'd reached safety, those men would continue to come for us. They would want to punish us for taking this boy. This would never be over. I elbowed her out of the way, grabbed the wheel and accelerated.

She stumbled back and fell to the floor. After a moment Catherine rushed toward me, then she wrestled my hands off the wheel. She was a force when she wanted to be, overtaking me and anyone else on a whim. "Slow down!"

For the first time in our shared existence I fought her with all I had and we wrestled for control.

The impact was abrupt, jarring and loud. There was no holding on and we flew through the air. My screams mixed with hers and it was in that split second, a moment that stretched and slowed to minutes, that it came back to me. That nagging thing I couldn't place sooner.

We were in our father's boat, pulling up to the restaurant with the neon pelican. I stared at the dark blue water in the distance while our father eased the boat into the slip.

"What's that?" I asked, pointing to a long line of huge black rocks and concrete jutting far into the water.

"A jetty," my father answered. "It protects the coastline."

I landed on what felt like cement, and it was only when I inhaled salty water into my lungs that I realized I was in the ocean. Searing pain shot through every inch of my body. I swam as hard as I could with my wrists still taped together, fighting for air. I finally got above water and there was an explosion. Intense heat and pain slashed my body.

Flames raged and grabbed at me and all I could do was scream, "Catherine!"

FORCED PERSPECTIVE CHAPTER 1
TWENTY YEARS LATER

T he shape of a man glided across the security monitor, his shadowy form dark and shifting. I threw my book aside and quickly turned off the light on the bedside table.

2:53 a.m.

No one should have been outside my house at this hour.

That camera view was from the upper left-hand corner of my small front porch. I watched him pull and push the handle of the locked front door.

I scrambled from the cool comfort of my bed and grabbed the air pistol from the top of the white fireplace mantel. I felt my way along the walls of the dark hallway. The renovation was ongoing and sconces hadn't yet been hung. The painting cloths were soft beneath my bare feet and I did a careful climb along the narrow half-spiral stair-case to the top level. I pressed myself against the wall since the workers hadn't installed the railing.

Quietly, I opened the door to the rooftop, stepped quickly to the south side, and peered over the edge that faced East York Street.

He blended into the night with his dark pants, dark T-shirt, and dark shoes. Straight dark hair poked out from beyond his black baseball cap.

It had been twenty years since the Muñoz crime family kidnapped us, since they kept us in cages, since they tried to kill us. So what I should have seen in this wannabe intruder was a local criminal. Someone who wanted something for nothing. But what I saw was someone from the Muñoz family, someone who would never forget what I'd done.

He pulled hard on each set of bars that covered my first-floor windows.

I silently thanked God that I'd finally finished that install two days ago. A lawyer from the firm next door tried to dissuade me from putting them in, said the bars detracted from the original beauty of the house. While I was a fan of form over function—any historical preservation project made you that way—I was a bigger fan of being safe.

The guy stood back, stared at my house, like there must've been a way for him to get inside. He crept around the side, his movements sleek and catlike.

I followed him until I stood at the very far corner of my roof and aimed the air pistol at him, but my angle didn't give me a good shot. So I waited. Followed him with my gun while he worked his way around to every first-floor window of my four-story home.

I'd been shooting at targets since I was thirteen. The owner of the first range I visited said he preferred their customers to be at least fourteen. But they made an exception for me because they knew what I'd been through.

The man who searched for easy access into my house had a half-inch waistband of white underwear sticking out at the back of his dark pants. That's where I aimed. I waited for him to make a move.

The all-too-familiar pressure built in my chest. Panic tightened every muscle, convincing me to act first, think later. Memories flashed like disco lights: the man who told Diego, the black-toothed man, to kill Catherine and me. The boat crash, the death threats and the attempts on my life that followed the trial.

I tried to blink the memories away. But twenty years after the kidnapping, my every reaction to a new threat was still a raw and primal fear that the Muñoz family had found me. I tightened my grip on the trigger.

The therapists had said to simply let the memories flow, not to fight them. That one day they would run their course, that time would tame them. That was easier said than done. Because the emotion in those memories ran strong enough to drown me. No amount of tears, no amount of feeling could alleviate the pain or the anger over what I'd lost.

I rubbed my eyes, squinted, flexed my hand several times.

The man checked under flower pots, ran his hand above the shutters and window frames like he searched for a hidden key.

"Come on in." I adjusted my bead on him. "Please."

As if he heard me, he pulled a short metal bar from under his pant leg, smashed the window glass through the bars. My house alarm blared, but he didn't move. The noise didn't even startle him. Like he expected it. He stepped close to the broken window, looked inside, then backed away.

I raised my head from my pistol aim and watched him.

He turned. Slowly, like he moved through deep water. Until he faced me. Like he knew where I was, like he knew I was watching.

Icy dread hit my chest.

Then I saw it, the faint glimmer of white teeth. A smile.

We each stood there, facing one another.

His knowing smile taunting me.

Sudden fury burned away the icy dread and I aimed for center mass.

Without a flinch in his greedy smile, he spun around and ran toward Columbia Square. Fast from the start.

I pulled the trigger.

He dodged to the right and the pellets hit the street sign with a loud metallic ding. He turned the corner. I dashed to the other side of the roof and looked over the side.

He wasn't down below.

He must have cut down E. President Street, half a block over.

My cell phone buzzed. It was the alarm company. I told them I was fine, that it looked like someone broke one of my windows. I reminded them I had bars on all my first-floor windows, I told them I didn't need any assistance.

I sat down, leaned against the half wall that surrounded the rooftop and tried to catch my breath. Adrenaline surged and prickled my skin like I'd swallowed a beehive.

I turned off the alarm from my phone, my hands shaking. The desire to run, pack everything and leave was overwhelming, stronger than a bad drug.

As an adult, I'd never lived in one place for more than a few months. I'd only worked consulting jobs that required lots of travel. I'd never owned a permanent residence.

Until now.

I pressed my palms against my eyes, and I saw the man's smile broaden in my mind.

He'd looked right at me. Knew where I was, knew where I'd be.

I looked up at the stars, drew in a deep inhale.

I should have shot him.

I put the gun next to me. Exhaled short and quick. It was impossible that they could have found me. I'd been too good, too careful. I'd changed my name, my hair and my eye color. I'd moved too many times to count.

I made a plan to review the security camera feed, to see if there were any clear shots of his face. If there were, I would study them, memorize his features. I would send the photo to Agent Hernandez, who could determine if the image matched anyone in his files.

I raised up to a half crouch and searched for signs of movement. Somewhere out there were the men who still wanted me dead.

I examined the softly moving shadows and wondered if anyone could see me.

With my vision at 20/15, I saw all things more clearly than most. As an antique jewelry restorer and authenticator, my eyes were trained to notice tiny details that others missed. What was subtle or invisible to someone else was glaring and obvious to me.

I remained still, only my eyes shifting, combing the area. On the west side of the house, gas lamps flickered, casting a weak yellow glow into the green space of Columbia Square. Every house on the square was dark, except Bunny's, my neighbor across the green.

She paced in her lamplit front room, wearing a long, white nightgown. Her gray-blond hair that was normally tied up in a twist was loose and long and almost reached her waist.

The bells of St. John the Baptist Cathedral struck three, their full, rich tones lingering in the night air. 3 a.m. was the cusp of the Witching Hour. "That hour between 3 and 4 a.m. is when the veil between the living and dead is at its weakest," Bunny had told me once.

I wasn't surprised to see her awake at this hour. Bunny was a wealthy widow whose husband's absence surrounded her like a black shawl, like a cloud, like the invisible man who never left her side. She'd been to many a seance at 3 a.m. trying to contact her dead husband. Once I went with her. But all I saw was a fair amount of money given in exchange for an infusion of hope porn.

The past was dead.

So was her husband.

At the sound of the bells she stopped pacing, went to the bay window, looked out into the night. She took her dead husband's gold wedding band that she kept on a chain around her neck, held it to her mouth and kissed it. She struck a long match and lit ten ivory-colored candles, five to her left, five to her right. Then turned out the singular lamp. She faced her front windows and kneeled and pressed her husband's ring between her palms. She rocked back and forth, her lips moving nonstop like she recited a chant.

I didn't think she would get what she was looking for.

I pushed away from the ledge.

With the wannabe intruder nowhere in sight, I decided to go downstairs and look at the security feed. I headed toward the door. A movement on the other side of the park caught my attention. I crouched again quickly, this time to all fours.

I crawled back to the short wall and stood halfway. I kept one hand tight on my pistol. If the intruder was back, I'd shoot him. I wouldn't hesitate.

But it wasn't him. I squinted. Chills scattered up my back and down my arms. Because the movement I'd seen wasn't a person. It wasn't an animal. But it looked alive. A low, rolling fog that crept and clawed its way between the Davenport and Kehoe houses.

Opaque and gray, it snaked onto the grassy park, moving with darkness and purpose until it overtook all four corners of the square. A shiver built inside of me and I tightened every muscle to hold it down.

There was no breeze in the square, but a coolness brushed against my face. A young woman emerged from the fog.

A spirit.

A ghost.

She wore a red spaghetti strap dress that flared at the hem, giving the illusion that she wore a light crinoline. Halfway across the grass she stopped. She peered into the fountain like she saw her own reflection. Her light brown hair fell over her shoulders in loose ringlets. She stood upright, turned and looked directly at me.

I caught my breath. I leaned forward. I clutched the wide cement edge in front of me. My heart drummed and I heard pounding in my ears.

I was so taken by her beauty I couldn't take my eyes off of her. Even if I didn't have my scars she would still have been the prettier one. I'd always known that, but tonight I couldn't stop staring. It wasn't envy, not anymore, anyway. She was just stop-and-stare stunning.

As a child she had been incredibly beautiful. In public, when onlookers compared us, they had a hard time concealing their reaction. The differences were minor, but obvious. I was a slightly watered-down version of her startling good looks.

She was older now. As twins, of course, we were the same age when she died. Only twelve. Now, twenty years later, we were still the same age. Apparently you grew up in Heaven, too.

She was as tall as I was. If we stood next to one

another our heights could have been exact. Her hair was the same length as mine, probably also exact. We still looked remarkably alike. Except she didn't have my scars. And I'd darkened my hair considerably, while her hair remained its natural light brown. Her eyes were our God-given crystal blue mine were covered with dark brown contacts.

There was my life before the kidnapping. There was my life now. The only thing that connected the two were my conversations with Catherine. They were quiet, existed only in my mind, and they were continual. Because even after I'd killed her, I still needed to tell her everything.

"Is it really you?" I whispered.

Her eyes held my gaze for a long moment.

"Are you angry with me?" I was certain she would be, for taking her life.

She smiled, and I wondered if she understood.

Her hand swept low into the fog and brought up a dandelion. Grasping it tightly between both hands, she closed her eyes. Her lips flattened into a wince. Like she was poised to make a wish, and she needed it to come true more than she needed life.

She pursed her lips and blew the downy tufts into the air. When she opened her eyes again, she watched the seeds travel, then land.

"What did you wish for?" I asked, breathless from my out-of-control heart.

She stared at me but didn't give an answer. She just walked back to the fountain, like she couldn't say or that the answer was mine to discover.

I worried for her, as I had since the night she left my life. Was she safe, was she hurting, did she hate me for what I'd done?

You are still my best friend, my confidant, my twin. You have always been, and will forever be, a part of me.

She blew me a kiss.

Her love flooded my insides like warm sunshine, and that Wonder Woman kind of confidence I'd only ever felt with her filled me, strengthened me, made me invincible.

I've forgotten things about us since you died. But not our connection, not the completeness, not the way you made me feel. Never that. Maybe because we shared one womb. Maybe because we were together at the beginning of our time. Maybe because the mind, the body, and the soul can't forget that kind of deep connection.

Whatever the reason, even death didn't stop the sense of home and belonging we always had with one another.

She took two steps toward me and stopped.

Stared hard.

Last time I saw that intense concern on her face I was racing her toward certain death.

She was worried. Not at peace. A dull ache pulled at my heart.

Was she really here?

Savannah was a city that lent itself to afterlife magic. All the locals said the veil between this world and the next was thinner here than anywhere else. Not just during the Witching Hour, but always. Spirits came and went all the time here, perhaps for no particular reason other than they could.

That was possible. Even probable. But Catherine's presence felt intentional. Deliberate. Like there was a reason for her visit.

Wait.

Was this even real?

I looked across the green, where Bunny stood in the

front room of her antebellum home, seemingly in conversation with someone I couldn't see. I was tempted to think she was nuts.

But there stood Catherine, clear as day. I knew what it was like to love someone so deeply, so perfectly, so completely, that you couldn't let go. No matter what.

I reached for my sister. My knuckles ached, stiff from gripping the edge.

She turned away. The low fog rolled up slowly from the north end of the square and curled in her direction.

Old guilt, black and shifting, as poisonous as any water moccasin, slithered up from dark places within. It was born when I crashed the boat. Tonight it crept around my heart and squeezed, crushing with a strength I didn't like, and a strength I couldn't calm.

The fierce inner combat between the loss I carried in my heart—that insistent part of me that wanted to make everything right—and the other equally insistent side of me—the part that knew I could never make it right—brought angry tears to my eyes.

She returned her haunted gaze to me, pointed three times to a silver watch on her left wrist, like she was saying, "It's time."

"Time?" I asked. "What time? Time for what?"

The moving fog ushered her away and to the south, my left, and out of Columbia Square. It parted where she stepped, her bare feet pale in the muted light of the street-lamps. Her long brown hair trailed behind her in the gentle, imaginary breeze.

When she reached the end of the green, she stopped, turned toward me. She gave me a sad smile, a worried smile, a too-many-burdens-on-her-heart smile. The fog caught up to her and she disappeared into the fading mist.

Columbia Square was empty.

My heart ached in my sister's absence. The fierceness I'd been armed with earlier melted under the weight of my grief.

I fell to my knees and sobbed.

AFTER A LONG TIME I finally dragged myself from the roof. I went down to the main level and brewed a pot of coffee. Magnolia, the neighborhood cat who claimed me when I moved in, swished her fluffy-soft tail against my legs, looked up and meowed. I opened the glass jar of treats on the counter, took out two and put them on the floor for her.

I reached for a mug from the small cabinet, my hand paused at the multitude of prescription bottles. The nurse would come by in the morning to dole out a few of each: Anti-impulsivity meds, anti-anxiety meds, anti-depressants, anti-everything meds. My parents, mostly my father, had pushed these prescriptions on me since the accident.

I hadn't expected them. Although I took them. Because in the beginning, I hadn't had a choice. Also because they worked. They lifted the depression, lowered the anxiety, dulled the other pain my father had caused. Made it easier to cope. But over the years, I took them off and on. More off than on because I hated the way they numbed me out.

Taken as prescribed they did banish the past. And they quieted that paranoiac voice to a far back corner, the one that said the Muñoz family was still out to get me.

But they didn't rid it entirely. And in exchange for that partial relief, the meds took something sacred away from me —my ability to feel. Really feel.

With each pill, a thick, wool sweater covered my brain

and heart, muting my thoughts and melting my feelings into lukewarm nothingness. I could no longer feel the ups and downs of life. I became a mushy middle ground—neither here nor there. Certainly no longer angry. Which meant I was no longer a problem to my father.

I never knew just how much I needed to feel my way through life until I couldn't. Those silent nudges, those internal checks that helped me feel which choices would work and what ones wouldn't, who was on my side and who wasn't—I needed those feelings.

I told my father and the doctors that I didn't need the meds anymore. But they insisted that I continue to take them, arguing that my feelings couldn't be trusted, that they were faulty indicators. They said that if I was left unmedicated, I was at risk of making bad decisions. Really bad decisions. They said my bad decisions could hurt someone.

What they didn't know was that they were wrong. Many of those meds I never needed. There were a few I benefitted from, and I took those. But I didn't need them anymore. I was better now.

I pulled my hand away from the bottles and doubled down on my recent decision not to take any of them anymore. When the nurse came in the morning I would do as I'd learned I could when I was much younger. I would pretend to take the pills so that she would give my father a good report. Then, after she left I would pull them from the back of my cheek and spit them down the drain.

I'd had my wisdom teeth taken out at thirteen, and that procedure left two gaps behind my upper molars. Those gaps in the back of my mouth came in handy for hiding tiny pills.

I grabbed my favorite mug, poured the coffee, added a

splash of cold milk. Stirred and sipped. I walked to the front bay window and stared into Columbia Square.

Bunny's house was now dark like all the others. Live oak branches and Spanish moss hung still in the damp summer heat. The nostalgic flame of the gas lamps and the bubbling fountain were the only signs of life.

I thought about the doctors' insistent warnings that going off the meds would cause hallucinations. But I'd done my research and I knew that staying on those meds carried a risk of hallucinations, too. As well as psychosis. Neither prospective scenario gave me comfort, so I had to be my own best advocate when it came to my health.

The park was empty.

Haunted.

Catherine's expression was burned into my mind and it wasn't soothing. If she'd visited me at all, and I wasn't certain that she had, she wasn't here to comfort me.

She was worried.

I wondered what she knew that I didn't.

Click here to continue the adventure with FORCED PERSPECTIVE today!

ALSO BY ALYSSA RICHARDS

THE FINE ART OF DECEPTION SERIES

THE FINE ART OF DECEPTION, UNDOING TIME

SOMEWHERE IN TIME

LOST IN TIME

THE FINE ART OF DECEPTION, BOXED SET

THE ALCOTT MANOR SERIES

THE HAUNTING AT ALCOTT MANOR

A MURDER AT ALCOTT MANOR

A STRANGER AT ALCOTT MANOR

THE CHASING SECRETS SERIES

CHASING SECRETS

FORCED PERSPECTIVE

Be the first to know about Alyssa Richards' next novel, sign up here: www.AlyssaRichards.com

and follow her on Amazon or BookBub to receive a new release alert!

ABOUT THE AUTHOR

ALYSSA RICHARDS is the USA TODAY BESTSELLING AUTHOR of romantic suspense and mystery thriller novels. She loves living in the South with her husband and two children. She also loves good espresso, her rescue dogs, magnolias and gardenias, and, of course, reading a great book. She grew up running barefoot in the Blue Ridge Mountains of North Carolina, where her favorite weekly adventure was a trip to the library with her mom.

Sign up for Alyssa's newsletter at www.alyssarichards.com to receive special offers, and news about her latest releases.

For More information
www.AlyssaRichards.com
Contact Alyssa at:
authoralyssarichards@protonmail.com

instagram.com/alyssaauthor

amazon.com/Alyssa-Richards/e/B00S1IGJ9O

bookbub.com/authors/alyssa-richards

goodreads.com/alyssarichards

ACKNOWLEDGMENTS

With gratitude to...

    ...my husband for his encouragement and belief in me.

    ...G & G for their loving support.

    ...my editor Peter Senftleben, who is amazing.